PUFFIN BOOKS

MABEL JONES
JONES
and the
FORBIDDEN
CITY

Will Mabbitt writes. He writes in cafes, on trains, on the toilet, and sometimes, when his laptop runs out of power, he writes in his head. He lives with his family somewhere in the south of England.

Ross Collins grew up with an affinity for drawing, the bionic man and precariously swinging backwards on chairs. Finding it hard to make a career from either of the latter two, he continued drawing and has since written and illustrated many award-winning books. Ross resides in Glasgow, Scotland.

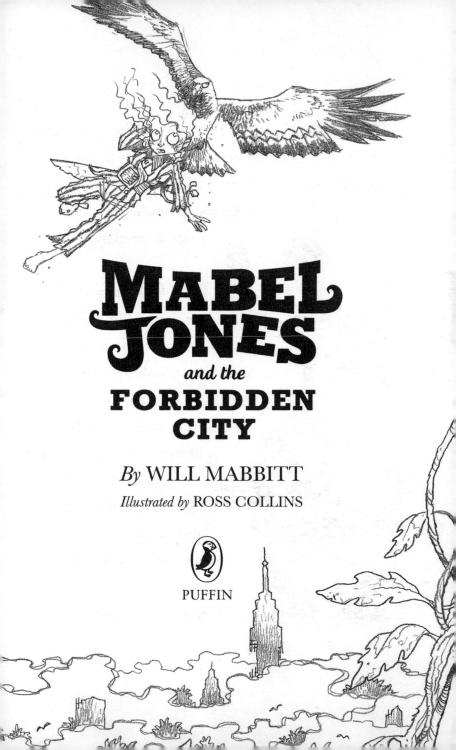

MABEL JONES
and the
FORBIDDEN CITY

By WILL MABBITT

Illustrated by ROSS COLLINS

PUFFIN

PUFFIN BOOKS

UK | USA | Canada | Ireland | Australia
India | New Zealand | South Africa

Puffin Books is part of the Penguin Random House group of companies
whose addresses can be found at global.penguinrandomhouse.com.

puffinbooks.com

First published 2016
001

Text copyright © Will Mabbitt, 2016
Illustrations copyright © Ross Collins, 2016

The moral right of the author and illustrator has been asserted

Text design by Mandy Norman
Printed in Great Britain by Clays Ltd, St Ives plc

A CIP catalogue record for this book is available from the British Library

ISBN: 978–0–141–35532–0

Penguin Random House is committed to a
sustainable future for our business, our readers
and our planet. This book is made from Forest
Stewardship Council® certified paper.

For Tilly, Etta and Ellen

CONTENTS

MAP *of the* NOO WORLD

the flight of Sir Cudeon Scapegrace

EVEN MORE IMPENETRABLE JUNGLE

GREAT MURKY RIVER

MARYVALE HIGH SCHOOL

This Area Particularly Rife with Tropical Bumrot

?

The FORBIDDEN CITY
X

IMPENETRABLE

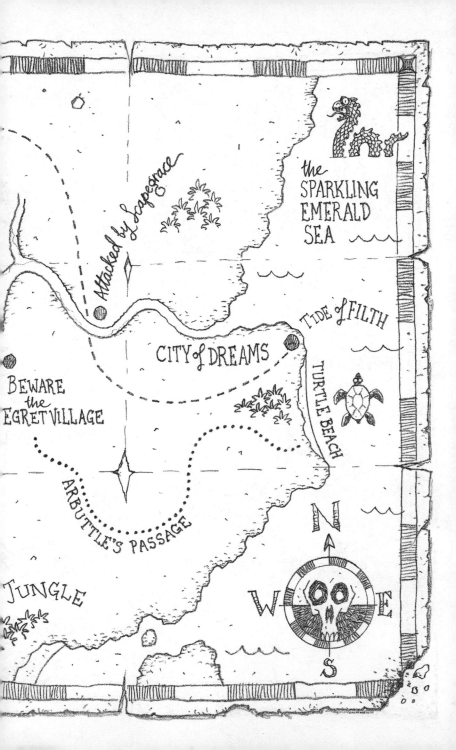

CHAPTER ONE
Fetch Her, My Foul Creepers

*M*abel Jones scratched her armpit thoughtfully and peered through the bars at the **extraordinary** creature before her.

It's a funny-looking thing, all wrinkled and fat and helpless. Like a beetle grub. Kind of slimy, but kind of cute too.

Her baby sister, Maggie, snored gently and blew a snot bubble from her left nostril.

Babies can be quite disgusting, thought Mabel, absent-mindedly picking her own nose and

wiping her finger on the wall. Especially when you have to share a bedroom with one.

She yawned, climbed into bed and fell asleep, totally unaware that something quite **dreadful** was about to occur.

Which (of course) is why *we* are here.

Slide open the window and **squeeze** inside.

I think we're just in time. We wouldn't want to miss any dreadfulness.

Creep silently to the wardrobe and **press** your gristly earhole trimmings to the door. Can you hear the distant sound of drumming?

A **frenzied** beat.

It grows **louder** and **louder** still!

What's this? **Chanting too?**

Just when I thought it couldn't get any worse. This must be some kind of witchcraft.

I don't like this. I don't like this one bit.

Far, far away, a long fingernail scrapes along the words of a letter – a letter written during a previous, **most unlikely** adventure by the very same Mabel Jones we see now safe and snug, asleep in her room. A letter bottled and corked and thrown over the side of a pirate ship into the rolling seas. For months it bobbed on those waves, years maybe, until it washed up on a far-away beach to be found, swapped, sold, stolen, then lost and found again, before it finally reached the hands of this strange and wicked creature.

Cracked and painted lips silently mouth the words of the letter. Then the fingernail pauses as it reaches the end of the final sentence, where an accidental memento has been left.

A single hair – a Mabel hair – is carefully removed from the letter and sniffed.

Fresh snuglet . . .

Fresh enough for dark magic.

The grim smile widens to reveal ancient crumbling teeth. The drumming has stopped. The chanting has died to a soft murmur. And now a voice speaks, in soft yet cracking tones – like honey poured thick on burnt toast – whispering an incantation:

'Fetch her, my foul creepers. Bring me the one called Mabel Jones . . .'

So brace yourself – for a wicked seed has been planted and, though its roots are firmly embedded in the future, its shoots and vines are winding through the hot and steaming mists of time into the present.

Quickly! Press your puny weight against those wardrobe doors, child. You must prevent this foulness from occurring.

Alas, it is futile. Your scrawny body is no match for the strength of dark magic.

It's time for the secret weapon. Have you brought the powdered beak of a heartbroken swan? Quickly mix it with your vial of hedgehog tears to make a paste, then mark the sacred sign upon –

What?

You don't have either of these things?

Really?

Really, really?

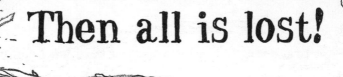

Then all is lost!

A thin white shoot sprouts through the gap between the wardrobe doors. It grows fast and strong, and splinters the wood. A vine has formed.
The vine branches.
Its branches branch.

Then those branches branch some more branches.

And the branches of the branches of the branches branch once more until the room is filled with curling vines that wrap and twist round bookcases and chair legs, pulling all they find closer to the open doors of the wardrobe, like the tentacles of a **starving octopus**.

Up the walls they creep . . .

Across the ceiling they wind . . .

All searching for one thing.

Fetch her, my foul creepers.

They reach the bed.

Bring me the one
called Mabel Jones!

A vine curls beneath the duvet, questing for the sleeping Mabel contained within.

Gripping round her ankles.

Tightening round her wrists.

Then with evil purpose the creepers tuck the duvet into place. Mabel is wrapped up, still snoring, like a sausage roll made with girl instead of pig parts. And slowly but surely the bundled snuglet is pulled towards the wardrobe.

Who knows what lies in store for a young girl stolen from her bed by the foul creepers of an evil enchantress?

Could this be the end for Mabel Jones?

A toe poking from beneath the duvet catches on a line of thread stretched tight above the floor, looped round a nail hammered into the skirting board, then stretched upward and tied to a precariously balanced tin of coppers.

KERCHANGaCHANG!!!

A booby trap! Set by clever,
resourceful Mabel Jones. She has had some
experience of unlikely adventures such as these. If
you have been snatched from your bedroom once,
then it pays to take great care it never happens
again.

Mabel Jones was woken by a sudden noise.

She had been having a strange dream that
she was being dragged into the wardrobe by
the tendrils of an evil creeping vine. Then she
realized it wasn't a nightmare.

It was **really happening**.

She opened her mouth to scream, but a thick
vine covered her face, smothering her cry for help.
Mabel, a skilled vegetarian, bit down hard and
tore off a fleshy chunk of plant with her teeth.

Vile and bitter sap filled her mouth, like she
had just swigged on a bottle of nit lotion. The
bitten vine recoiled, spilling sap on the bedroom
carpet.

Mabel bit another vine and her arm was free. Free enough to grab a nearby shoe and use it to hammer at the vines that dragged her towards the wardrobe. Vine by vine she fought the plant, until she was sitting in a pool of mushed and mangled stems. The creepers were retreating now, shrinking back into the wardrobe. The spell was broken.

Mabel sat panting in the remains of her bedroom.

My name is Mabel Jones, and I am not scared of anything.

But something is wrong, Mabel.

Something precious is missing.

Something very precious indeed.

'My matchbox full of toenail clippings!'

Four years' work – gone.

And something else, Mabel?

'Oh, and the cot is empty.'

MAGGIE IS GONE!

Mabel's sister, sleeping soundly, stood no chance. Plucked from her cot and dragged into the wardrobe, along with a Tupperware box of Lego, Mabel's recorder and, of course, the toenail-clipping collection.

Look!

The final vine is disappearing back into the wardrobe! Mabel leaps to stop it. Maggie Jones may well be a slightly inconvenient and annoying baby sister, but she is *Mabel's* slightly inconvenient and annoying baby sister.

Mabel grabs the vine and for a moment she holds it fast.

'GIVE. ME. BACK. MY. SISTER!'

Then the vine tugs, sudden and swift, and Mabel falls forward into the wardrobe – into a hot, steaming mist, her fingers still gripped round the end of the tendril.

Somewhere in the distance, the familiar sound of a wailing baby can be heard.

MAGGIE!

Then the vine snaps, weakened by the earlier bites of the desperate Mabel Jones.

And

she is fal*ling*

. . .

Falling away from the cries of her baby sister . . . **Falling into darkness.**

And then, with a thump, she is back in her wardrobe!

Actually, this isn't my wardrobe . . .

This is the inside of a **completely different** wardrobe!

CHAPTER TWO
The City of Broken Dreams

*I*f you sail across the **WILD WESTERN SEA** until
the water warms and turns an emerald
green, you will eventually reach a land that
stretches as far north, and as far south, as the eye
can see.

Welcome to the **NOO WORLD**.

So anchor your ship, drop a dinghy in the
gentle waves and row to the beach.

And when you're there let us wallow in the
warm shallows together.

Let us paddle among the reefs, collecting the
shells of conches and giant clams.

Let us frolic on the white beach and climb the palms to pick green coconuts and forage for plump dates.

Let us lie in the dappled shade of the lush forest that lines the shore and watch as this rare turtle breaks the surf, preparing to flap up the beach to gently lay her eggs in the same sun-warmed sand where she herself hatched all those years ago.

The circle of life is complete!

Well, almost complete.

Start the barbecue. Pull up a log. For there will be enough turtle for everyone! I bagsy a flipper.

Ah, this is the life! Do you mind greasing my back? The bald bits need special attention, for I am cursed with **mange** and my patchy fur does not fully protect me from the sun's harmful rays. I actually have *very* delicate skin.

But what is that awful smell that taints the salty breeze?

Look! A slick in the *Sparkling Emerald Sea* – a swirling mass of greasy water and floating scraps, brought to the beach courtesy of the gentle waves. The turtle pauses, then returns to the sea. Her sacred birthing beach has been spoilt. And our delicious main course has left.

So let us follow this slick to its source, some miles along the coast, where the jungle gives way to the stench, sickness and hot, dry smog of a city – a sprawling mess of narrow litter-strewn streets and hastily constructed houses that lean against each other for support.

Its population? A motley mix of **adventurers**, *romantics* and **criminals**, all arriving to seek their fortune in the **NOO WORLD**.

See them at the docks, wheeling their suitcases from the tramp steamers and cargo vessels that have sailed across the **WILD WESTERN SEA**. Whether they be fox, or deer, or bear, or shrew, all have

the same dream: to start anew in a land of limitless opportunity.

And the sparkling light that draws them in? Why, it is the twinkle of DIAMONDS! For it is whispered in the cities of the OLD WORLD that this distant shore positively rattles with the wonderful stones.

And so these hopeful travellers stream from the ships' gangways, funnelled to the city's numerous boarding houses, hotels and taverns. Places such as the **HOTEL PARADISO** – the filthiest muck-hole in the whole rotten manure-heap of a city.

Press upon the bell if you dare. Push past the cat that opens the door. Be careful not to brush against him, for he is ridden with tropical fleas and prone to uncontrollable bouts of **spraying**. Step over the drunken porter. It is best that he does not help us with our bags, for the young whippet is a dishonest sort and light of paw. He'd suck the mayonnaise from your tuna sandwich given a moment alone with your lunch box.

DO NOT
TAKE
THE LIFT!

It has been deliberately stopped between the second and third floors by a rabid shrew who refuses to pay his board. He screams blue murder through the night.

Instead, climb the rickety stairs to the third floor.

Step carefully over the cowpat that has been deposited upon the landing carpet by a disgruntled guest – a dirty protest at the bad service received during his unhappy stay – and then into room 16b (the King Charles Honeymoon Suite), where we wait for the story to continue. For contained within this room, inside a badly constructed and wormholed wardrobe, is poor confused sisterless Mabel Jones . . .

The wardrobe door opened out on to a small and WONKY-looking bedroom with a double bed and a small broken window. Mabel cautiously stepped into the bright sunlight that shone through the dirty glass. Some cockroaches that had been basking on mildewed and dribble-stained pillows scuttled under the filthy sheets for safety.

There was a knock on the door and a bleary-eyed young whippet looked in. 'Post for room 16b.'

He held out two envelopes.

Mabel blinked. 'Thank you,' she said.

The whippet shrugged. 'No money or nuffin. I shook 'em to check.'

Mabel blinked again. Then she smiled to herself. 'I think I'm on *another* unlikely adventure.'

She had returned to the future. A future with *no*

humans. A future with talking animals! A future she knew well, for she had been here before. In fact, last time she was here . . .

Well, that's a different story.

But the fact remained: Mabel Jones was alone. The only reminder of her own time was a half-empty paper bag of jelly babies in her pyjama pocket.

Mabel looked at the envelopes. Maybe they could give her some clue to where in the future she was?

Sir Timothy Speke
The Hotel Paradiso
City of Dreams
The Noo World

Carruthers Badger-Badger
The Hotel Paradiso
City of Dreams
The Noo World

Mabel's brow furrowed.

The Noo World? I don't even know where the old one is!

A noise came from outside: a ragged and tuneless voice raised in song.

'*I took a fancy to pox-ridden Nancy but she . . . errr . . .*'

The voice tailed off as the singer tried to remember the next line.

Mabel absent-mindedly pocketed the envelopes in her pyjamas and walked over to open the window.

The first thing she noticed was the **heat** – a dry, dusty heat that clung to the inside of her mouth as if she'd just drunk a glass of sand.

The second thing she noticed was that she was on the third floor of a rather badly built building, in a narrow street of similarly badly built buildings. One end of the street merged into a sprawling mess of a city, while the other opened out on to a view of a beautiful green sea.

The last thing she noticed was that on a balcony across the street stood a beaver in

dirty underpants.

He grinned a
gap-toothed
grin and
saluted her
with a half-
drunk bottle
of grog that
sloshed on to the
filth-strewn street
below.

'Good morning! *Guten Tag! Bonjour! Buenos días!*'

Mabel shielded her eyes from the bright
sunlight. 'Hi, I'm Mabel. Have you seen a plant
carrying a baby?'

The beaver laughed. 'I have never seen such a
sight! There are no plants here any more, for the
jungle has been burnt down to make space for the
CITY OF DREAMS, where the gutters are
strewn with ◆D◆I◆A◆M◆O◆N◆D◆S◆!'

He waved a paw around wildly, indicating the ramshackle building and filthy streets.

Mabel looked down. Some rats scampered across the road to forage for scraps from an upturned bin. She couldn't see any diamonds.

The beaver looked thoughtful. He had a kindly face. He leant on the rail, missed his handhold and slopped more drink over the edge of the balcony and on to the street below.

'But they say **Mr Habib** can answer any question you may think of, for the price of a single silver penny.'

'Where can I find Mr Habib?' asked Mabel.

'He lives in the Giblet-packing District. Opposite **Bogdan's Offal Stop**. Look out for his sign. But be warned . . .'

He paused for dramatic effect.

'Be warned of what?' asked Mabel. It sounded important.

The beaver looked confused.

'Erm . . . Be warned of . . .'

Suddenly he squealed with fright and jumped back into his room.

A gruff voice spoke from behind Mabel Jones. 'Put your hands up and turn round slowly. This is a **military revolver**, capable of discharging multiple rounds before reloading. The combination of its power and my marksmanship has been sufficient to take down a variety of assailants. We'll have no problems dispatching a common thief.'

Mabel turned round slowly. A squat badger was pointing a large pistol at her. Hiding behind the badger stood an otter peering nervously at her through a monocle.

'I say, CARRUTHERS, you fibber! We've only just bought that horrid gun, and you said yourself we need to read the instructions before using it!'

The badger glared at his companion. 'Be quiet, *Speke*! Can't you see I'm bluffing?'

'Golly! How cunning of you, Carruthers! Is it even *loaded*?' whispered the otter.

'For goodness' sake, be quiet!' hissed the badger. 'The thief may speak our language.'

The otter clapped his paws together in excitement. 'How wonderful!'

Mabel stepped forward, opening her mouth to explain the misunderstanding.

'You stay where you are!' ordered the badger, wobbling the pistol about in her direction.

Mabel hadn't been shot before, but in her previous unlikely adventure she'd seen both a good friend and a dastardly enemy mortally wounded by a bullet. She didn't fancy taking any chances.

'Check our belongings, Speke. Make sure this creature hasn't stolen the . . .' The badger paused. He eyed Mabel suspiciously. 'Make sure this creature hasn't stolen anything of importance.'

The otter scrabbled beneath the bed, pulled

out a briefcase and opened it.

'Still here,' he said, holding
up a bundle of old papers.
'Thank goodness!'

The badger
looked at Mabel
closely. 'It seems we
were just in time.
Truly, Speke, the
NOO WORLD has some
interesting species.
This shifty-eyed
burglar seems
to be some kind
of primate! An
ape, I'll warrant,
for it has no
visible tail. Yet it
lacks the sloping
brow and pleasant

demeanour of such a creature. A zoological mystery!'

'Would you like me to sketch it?' asked Speke, eagerly reaching for the suitcase again. 'For the society magazine?'

Mabel sighed impatiently. She was on important business. She didn't have time to sit for a portrait.

'Actually, I am *not* an ape *or* a monkey. I'm a girl.' She glared at the badger. 'AND I AM DEFINITELY NOT A BURGLAR.'

The two animals looked at each other.

'It does speak our language!' said the otter. 'What a charming accent!'

The badger frowned. 'Hide the bundle away from her, Speke, lest she glance upon anything that may betray our mission.'

'But, Carruthers, she couldn't possibly know it's a **treasure** map!'

Exasperated, the badger turned to face his

companion. 'Really, Timothy, you are *too* much.'

It was Mabel's chance. Spinning round, she ran for the open window. In one leap she was on the sill and in another she had jumped across the street to the balcony opposite. Then, pausing briefly to apologize to the beaver (who was now sitting on the toilet with the door open), she ran down the stairs, on to the street and away into the city.

Mabel Jones had business to attend to.

CHAPTER THREE
Spirits of the Dark and Fetid Undergrowth

Shhh!

There it is again.

The distant sound of drumming. A frenzied beat.

It gets **louder** and **louder** still!

Listen! That voice. It speaks again.

Soft but menacing, like splinters of broken glass hidden beneath the skin of a sweet and creamy rice pudding.

'Speak. Speak, spirits of the dark and fetid undergrowth. Where is the one called Mabel Jones?'

And in reply?

Just the whistle of wind through

ruined buildings ...

Just the rustle of ferns upon

shattered pavements ...

And if we were there (and be thankful we are not, but if we were), then we would see an ancient sorceress smile and translate the jungle's whispered words.

'She is on her way. The one called Mabel Jones is coming.'

Her grey, wrinkled lips, daubed with blood-red lipstick, would peel back from aging, yellowed teeth. Her cheeks, unused to such exercise, would shed the dry skin that crusts under thickly applied white face-paint.

What is this creature?

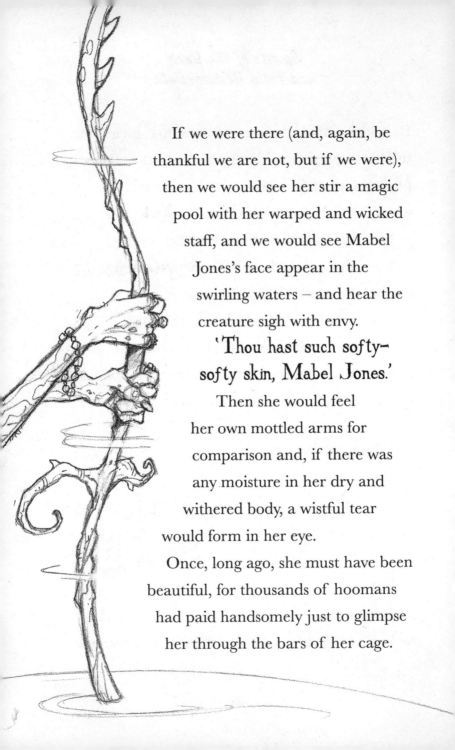

If we were there (and, again, be thankful we are not, but if we were), then we would see her stir a magic pool with her warped and wicked staff, and we would see Mabel Jones's face appear in the swirling waters – and hear the creature sigh with envy.

'Thou hast such softy-softy skin, Mabel Jones.'

Then she would feel her own mottled arms for comparison and, if there was any moisture in her dry and withered body, a wistful tear would form in her eye.

Once, long ago, she must have been beautiful, for thousands of hoomans had paid handsomely just to glimpse her through the bars of her cage.

Daily the crowds had trooped past her enclosure, their little ones pressing their faces to the fence. Occasionally, if the grown-up ones weren't watching, they would throw *sweeties*.

How she had loved those sweeties.

Even then, though, in those happier times, she had wished that she could be as they were. Shiny, pretty clothes. Smiling, furless faces.

And now, after thousands of years spent mastering the darkest of magic, she is almost ready. Ready to become hooman.

Not quite.

Not yet.

Soon, though.

Soon all the parts of the vile ceremony will be in place. All she will need then is the hooman child whose body she will take – she glances down at a shifting, snoring bundle, hidden deep in the folds of her silken gown. A bundle containing the baby, Maggie Jones. Not this one. Not this wriggling grublet. She needs a **real** child. An older child. For dark magic to work, its subject must contain at least a hint of bad, a pinch of naughty, or (whisper it) a teaspoon of wicked.

The creature strokes away a lock of fine hair from the sleeping babe's forehead.

Yes. This one is innocent. Too young to be truly bad. But its sister . . .

'I can sense it, Mabel Jones.

Something dark lurks deep inside thee.

And this little maggot will bring thee

right to me . . .'

CHAPTER FOUR
The Collector of Beaks

*N*ight had fallen on the **CITY OF DREAMS**, filling its labyrinth of alleyways and avenues with the kind of dangerous darkness that only the brave, or the exceedingly drunk, dare venture out in. A young hooman girl stepped warily through the filth-strewn streets. Leaping carefully over a puddle of blood that oozed from beneath the closed door of a ramshackle warehouse, Mabel Jones (for it is she, obviously) turned to inspect a tiny wooden shack that stood close by. Taking a deep breath, she tapped politely on the door.

The small window in the top of the door flapped open. A round, beady eye looked out.

'What do you want?' croaked a voice from inside.

'I'm looking for Mr Habib,' replied Mabel Jones. 'Does he live here?'

'Who wants to know?'

'I'm Mabel Jones. Pleased to meet you.'

The eye blinked. 'I've never heard of Mr Habib,' snapped the voice.

The small window closed. Mabel knocked again.

'Excuse me, but on the door . . .' She paused to read the crudely scratched sign out loud.

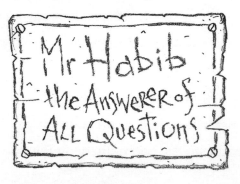

The window opened again. 'I'm not in!'

Mabel pushed her face close to the little window and peered through. A tiny monkey with long wispy eyebrows looked back at her.

It blinked. '*A hooman?*'

Mabel nodded.

The window closed. Mabel could hear the monkey muttering to himself inside.

'A hooman snuglet! *Very* rare. *Very* rare indeed. Oh my days, such a lucky, lucky monkey Mr Habib is!'

The door opened. 'Mr Habib will see you now,' said the monkey, fastening a filthy dressing-gown. He beckoned her with a jerk of his head. Inside was cramped, dark and dirty. Mabel could hardly see a thing.

Mr Habib ushered her in to sit on a cushion on the floor, then disappeared into a dark corner. There was rattling and jangling, and then an oil lamp was lit and the room flooded with light.

Mabel gasped.

Hanging on the walls were beaks.

Hundreds of beaks: large beaks, small beaks, beaks of all shapes and sizes.

All carefully removed from the faces of their former owners and mounted on wooden boards.

Mr Habib followed her gaze. 'Ah, you like Mr Habib's collection? The biggest in the world, perhaps?' He smiled proudly.

Mabel said nothing.

His eyes narrowed in suspicion. 'Have you seen bigger?'

Mabel shook her head.

'You have not been to the **SACRED MUSEUM OF BEAKS** in Otom?'

'No.'

'Good. It is not worth the admission fee once you have been inside **Mr Habib's Beak Emporium**.'

He pointed to a particularly savage-looking beak hanging on the wall.

'They do not have the beak of the carnivorous emu. Nor the beak of an octopus. Nor do they have a complete collection of Galapagan finch beaks.'

He opened his dirty dressing-gown to reveal a colourful array of tiny beaks hanging from strings like bunting.

'Oh, the beak is a wonderful thing, is it not? So many shapes and sizes and colours . . .'

His voice tailed off and his eyes took on a faraway look. Slowly, one of his little hands reached up towards Mabel's face. 'So many interesting specimens . . .'

Mabel took a step backwards, bumping into a cage that stood in a corner of the room. Squashed in the cramped cage was a large dark-blue bird. The bird returned Mabel's gaze with its beady black eyes. Then it **squawked**.

Mabel looked at Mr Habib. 'Who's this?'

The bird **squawked** again.

'It's like he's trying to tell me something . . .'

Mr Habib shuffled nervously and pulled a blanket over the cage.

'But you have not come to talk of the **rare blue buzzard** and its extremely valuable beak. You have a question for Mr Habib. And you have come to the right place, for Mr Habib knows everything.'

He pulled a tiny chair close to Mabel, sat
down, closed his eyes and began to hum.

Mabel waited.

Suddenly Mr Habib opened his eyes. He was
staring – staring past Mabel into an unknown
distance. He was in a **trance**.

'Ask Mr Habib your question.'

'Where is my little sister?' asked Mabel.

Mr Habib put his hand into a small
earthenware pot, pulled out a selection of small
white objects and cast them upon the table.

'The finger bones of my ancestors will answer!'

Mabel leant forward eagerly. 'And?'

Mr Habib's eyes rolled back in his head. His
arms flopped loosely at the sides of his body. For
a second, Mabel thought he was going to faint.
Then he began to speak.

His voice had changed. It was deeper. Far
deeper than you'd expect from a small monkey.

'Your sister is in **great danger**.'

Mabel gasped. 'Where is she?'

'I see a faceless figure, shrouded in a jungle mist. You have something she wants. I see an ancient tower that grows from the black and burnt earth of a **FORBIDDEN CITY**.'

Suddenly Mr Habib winced and put his hands up to protect his face.

'No! Great danger!
Her magic is strong.
Too strong for Mr Habib!'

He fell to the floor, writhing and sobbing. 'The **ultimate sacrifice** must be made. Only the pure of heart can defeat **dark magic**!'

Then he sat up.

'That'll be one silver penny, please.'

His voice had returned to normal.

Mabel put her hands in
her pyjama pockets and
turned them inside out.

'I'm afraid I don't
have any money. Just jelly
babies – and they're a bit covered in fluff.'

'No money? Very bad. Mr Habib does not
accept baby-fluff jelly.' He twiddled his thumbs
thoughtfully, then stopped. 'Mabel Jones pay in
other way.'

He turned away from Mabel and hunched
over the oil lamp.

A quiet hand dipped into a concealed pocket.
Sly fingers foraged for a handful of secret
herbs.

An unseen smile crept across his face as he
sprinkled them over the flame, and the room
began to fill with a sweet and sickly smell . . .

Mr Habib turned to face Mabel. Reaching
out his tiny paw, he stroked her hand. 'Mabel

Jones has something very valuable for Mr
Habib.'

Poor unknowing, trusting Mabel Jones shifted
awkwardly on her cushion. She was pretty sure
she didn't have anything of value.

'I should really be going . . .'

But the smell of the lamp was overpowering.

Why do I feel so tired?

'Mabel Jones feeling sleepy?' said Mr Habib.
'Mabel stay with Mr Habib a little longer.'

Mabel tried to stand.

So tired . . .
        Can't . . .
                get . . .
                        up . . .

She **Stumbled** to her knees.

Must stay awake . . .

Mr Habib reached out two bony fingers and pinched Mabel's nose. She tried to wriggle free, but it was as though she had no control of her body. Her eyelids were closing. The need for sleep was overwhelming.

Mr Habib grinned nastily.

He gave her nose a twist, and then tilted it to look up her nostrils. Then he jerked it to the left and the right. Finally he felt the top bit where the bone was.

'What a specimen. Even the **SACRED MUSEUM OF BEAKS** in Otom doesn't have a *hooman* beak!'

Slowly he reached beneath the blue buzzard's cage and pulled out a pair of rusting **iron shears**, clacking the blades together gleefully.

So that was how Mabel Jones's debt was to be repaid: her nose would adorn the walls of **Mr Habib's Beak Emporium**.

It would never be picked again!

CHAPTER FIVE
Fluffy Bunnies

O h, it is too much!
Avert your eyes from the gruesome spectacle.

Close this grisly book you read.

Close it at once, I say.

At once!

Hand it to a responsible adult to throw upon a bonfire. Unless it was borrowed from a library, in which case return it with a strongly worded letter of complaint (you wouldn't want to get a fine, for librarians are a callous breed that would send their own grandmothers to the poorhouse for an unpaid debt).

That's better. Now fetch a *nicer* book. I'll warm some milk while you toddle off for a copy of *Princess Pink Kitten's Birthday Picnic*. That's *much* safer. Or how about that one with the *fluffy bunnies* that love each other *very* much? No severed noses in that one either, I'll bet!

Bye-bye, then.

Sleep tight.

Kiss-kiss.

Love you all the way to the moon and back!

Good, they've gone. We've got rid of the pale-kidneyed readers who don't realize that with unlikely adventures must come great danger, and with great danger sometimes comes the loss of an appendage – in this case, **a nose!**

They can run home to their mummies to sob into their silky-soft handkerchiefs about the dreadful things they've read, while we continue with the story. So grit your teeth, furrow your brow and hold on to your tail, for the beak-shearing of Mabel Jones is upon us . . .

What's that you say?

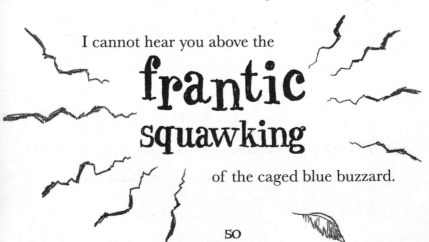

I cannot hear you above the

frantic
squawking

of the caged blue buzzard.

Mabel's eyelids are **flickering!**

Can the bird's warning squawks penetrate the stupefying fug of Mr Habib's soporific herbs?

Mr Habib opens the shears to their maximum width . . .

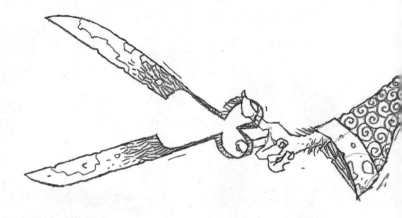

Mabel groans slightly.

Mr Habib tenses his muscles and steadies his hands. He needs a clean cut for a neat specimen . . .

The bird in the cage **squawks** again. It is a piercing shriek that shatters the fusty air,

and . . .

With a last-possible-nanosecond jerk of her neck, Mabel Jones pulled her nose away from the slicing blades of Mr Habib's shears.

Shaking her head to clear her fuzzy brain, she stumbled against the table and knocked it over. Burning oil spilled from the upturned lamp, filling the room with a choking smoke.

Fresh air! Need fresh air . . .

Mabel reached for the door, pushed it open and collapsed on to the street. She took a breath of cool, sweet night air. Slowly but surely her head cleared.

She looked up.

Next to her sat Mr Habib, watching his home burn. Large flames were jumping from the windows. Thick black smoke was climbing high into the sky.

Tears streamed down his face. 'My beaks, my beautiful beaks!'

Mabel stood up and brushed the dust from her pyjamas. She was safe. But something was wrong . . .

'The bird!' she cried.

Mr Habib's caged blue buzzard was still inside!

Without thinking, Mabel ran back into the burning building.

Through the thick smoke ...

Through the dancing flames ...

The cage was on the ground, trapped by a fallen timber and twisted out of shape. The buzzard lay motionless inside. Mabel reached in and carefully lifted him through the warped bars of the cage, ignoring the flames that licked round her feet and the smoke that choked her face holes.

Then, ducking another burning timber, she stooped through the door and ran back out into the street.

A crowd of creatures had spilled out from a nearby tavern and gathered to watch the fire. They clapped and cheered as Mabel reappeared, all singed and sooty.

She knelt and laid the unconscious bird on the street, unsure of what to do next. The crowd's cheering stopped as they saw the curled-up body.

The gap-toothed beaver she had spoken to earlier stepped forward. His simple, honest face was creased with worry. 'Is he dead?'

Mabel nodded, her eyes filling with tears. 'I think so.'

It seemed so unfair.

'If only I hadn't knocked over the table!'

A tear rolled down her cheek and fell on to the buzzard's face.

There was a soft squawk. Then the bird coughed and opened his eyes.

A rush of relief passed through Mabel. 'Are you OK?'

The buzzard looked at her, his beady black eyes betraying no emotion.

'**Squawk,**' he said.

Mabel sighed. 'I *wish* we could understand each other.'

The buzzard frowned.

'Well, maybe if you bothered to learn the

language before you came to a foreign country, you wouldn't have these problems,' he said haughtily. 'I'd *assumed* you could speak **Buzzard**.'

Then, without looking back, the magnificent bird wobble-ran down the street and took off with a loud flapping. Mabel watched as he circled once overhead then soared into the distance.

Slowly the crowd began to disperse, many of them following a strange meaty smell that led to the door of a bar on the opposite side of the street.

A kidney-shaped sign bore the title:

Mabel grimaced. She wasn't sure what offal was, but it certainly didn't smell good.

Then she saw it.

There in the front window – looking very out of place – was an immaculate handwritten sign.

Wanted

Intrepid Adventurers to join a Scientific Expedition to the Jungle Interior

Apply within

The Jungle Interior!

Mr Habib had spoken of a jungle mist. Maybe this expedition could be a way to find Maggie.

Popping a jelly baby into her mouth, Mabel Jones crossed the road and pushed open the rickety door of **Bogdan's Offal Stop**.

Dear Veronica,

I hope this letter finds you well.

We have arrived in the City of Dreams, Speke and I. The crossing was abominable and the city itself is hot, dry and riddled with the thieves, beggars and chancers that one would expect from abroad.

Tonight we set up table in Bogdan's Offal Stop, a grimy riverside bar, hoping to recruit porters and a boat with which to travel up the Great Murky River. This majestic waterway — the widest I have ever seen — winds its way into the jungle interior and, if my maps are to be believed, passes the Forbidden City: our expedition's goal.

Although no one from the Old World has ever travelled that far and lived to tell the tale!

Forgive me if I have frightened you, for such awfulness has no place in the delicate and simple mind of a lady. Enough expedition news, for my thoughts return to more serious matters.

Matters of the heart.

You see, Veronica, it has come to my attention that Speke is fond of you. Actually, he has told me as much: he read me one of his awful poems.

He appears to be of the mistaken opinion that his feelings are, if not completely then at least partially, returned by yourself. The thought of which fills me with dread,

Veronica. Because, although we have not known each other long, I feel a mutual admiration has built between us. By your own admission, you find me both 'boring' and 'predictable' — attributes upon which I pride myself, and also essential qualities for a husband.

In summary, you are a fine, healthy-looking creature, and I feel sure that, should this expedition be a success, I will be in a position to offer you a lifetime of financial stability.

Veronica, I am not prone to bouts of emotional behaviour but I cannot hold myself back any longer.

I like you.

Forgive my impudence.

Carruthers Badger-Badger, PhD

CHAPTER SIX
Bogdan's Offal Stop

LICENSED TO SELL INTOXICATED LIVERS

Bogdan's Offal Stop

NO CREDIT

STARTER
Offal* ~~2·00~~ 3·00

MAIN
Offal* ~~2·00~~ 3·00

PUDDING
Offal* ~~2·00~~ 3·00

*may contain nuts

114 Spleen Boulevard
Giblet-Packing District
City of Dreams
The Noo World

HYGIENE RATING
★ ☆ ☆ ☆ ☆
"Improved"

*M*abel returned the menu to the bar llama.
'Can I have a glass of tap water, please?'

The bar llama spat into a glass and wiped it clean with a filthy rag. 'Would you like some offal in that?'

Mabel shook her head, wondering what she would be doing if she were at home now. She'd probably be having dinner. Everyone would be fussing over Maggie, who would be mashing some over-boiled broccoli into the tablecloth.

Mr Habib's words echoed round her skull.

Your sister is in great danger . . .

What could that danger be?

I see a faceless figure, shrouded in a jungle mist . . . I see an ancient tower that grows from the black and burnt earth of a forbidden city.

Even though she was annoying sometimes, Maggie probably didn't deserve to be lost forever in the jungle. If nothing else, how would Mabel

ever explain it to her mum and dad? They seemed
very fond of Maggie.

Mabel sighed. There was no alternative. She
would have to find the ancient tower and get her
sister back, even if that *did* mean still sharing
her bedroom.

A familiar voice from across the bar caught
Mabel's attention. It was Speke, the otter from the
HOTEL PARADISO. Next to him sat the badger,
Carruthers, who was addressing a mysterious
stranger shrouded in a thick smog of pipe-smoke.

'I say, are you sure you're not a pirate?'

'Nay, I be an honest river boatman looking
for honest work. It sounds like my little paddle
steamer, the **BROWN TROUT**, would be just
right for yer expedition, she being perfectly suited
for cruising the **Great Murky River**. Certainly
there'll be no others willing to travel to –' the
mysterious stranger lowered his voice to a whisper
– '**THE FORBIDDEN CITY**.'

THE FORBIDDEN CITY!

Mabel looked up from her glass of water as the steamboat captain continued.

'They say it is an evil place, ruled by an all-powerful sorceress!'

Carruthers raised an eyebrow. 'Piffle! Mere superstition.'

'They say,' continued the captain, 'that the sound of her hideous howl can flatten palm trees, and that every living soul within a hundred miles of the **FORBIDDEN CITY** has been enslaved by her **dark magic**.'

'Unscientific codswallop!' scoffed the badger.

A pipe appeared from the cloud of smoke and jabbed towards Carruthers. 'Ye may say that, but I've been to ancient places before, and I says they be places where things happen, the like of which ye scientist types would never believe! So I'll take the job but I'll be wanting some **loot** up front . . .'

Speke looked at Carruthers, who grudgingly slid a small leather bag across the table to the smoke-shrouded captain.

Mabel couldn't wait a moment longer. She pushed her way over to the table.

'I'd like to join the expedition too, please.'

Speke looked up. 'Why, Carruthers, it's the girl from the hotel!'

The badger glared at Mabel. 'There's no place on this expedition for a girl, especially not a thieving one.'

Mabel ignored the grumpy badger and addressed the otter. '*Please*. My sister has been taken to the **FORBIDDEN CITY**. I need to rescue her!'

Speke looked at Carruthers imploringly through his monocle. 'It does sound jolly important.'

The badger frowned. 'Speke, she is nothing more than a common thief . . .'

'Well, our help could be what she needs – to save her from her life of crime.'

Carruthers looked at his friend sympathetically. 'Really, Speke, you are a kind-hearted simpleton. But I'm afraid a leopard cannot change its spots.'

A leopard sitting at a nearby table looked over crossly.

Carruthers nodded his head politely. 'No offence, madam.'

Then the captain spoke. 'As it happens, we *are* a crew member short. And those spindly fingers look perfect for the twiddling of fiddly valves. This puny snuglet may be a bald-faced bag of bones, but ye can't judge a shipmate by his beard – or lack thereof. I'll warrant this greenweed has seen many an **unlikely adventure** in her time.'

Mabel looked up at the captain. The fog from his pipe had cleared to reveal a plaited beard, a pair of dangerous-looking horns and a familiar grin.

It's funny how sometimes, when you're furthest away from home, you meet someone you know.

Mabel knew this goat.

A huge grin stretched across her face.

'PELF!'

And you may know him too, if you have read the first of Mabel's unlikely adventures – available to steal from all good bookshops (though I'd advise you to stay away from such places, as nothing dulls the mind like reading, and they tend to be staffed by the dreariest word-peddlers you could ever imagine).

For those of you who have not had the misfortune to read of Mabel's first adventure, I'd best describe Pelf. Time has passed since Mabel's last encounter with the veteran pirate – enough time for Pelf to have been added to the latest edition of the *Who's Who of Pirates* sticker album.

I have his sticker. Swapped for a duplicate of **Captain Matilda Smuts**, the ladymouse pirate of the **Cheese Coast**, scourge of the Edam trade and wanted in six countries for an incident involving the dumping at sea of an overripe Camembert during a royal swimming gala.

Here is Pelf's sticker:

362   362

PELF

FORMER FIRST MATE ON PIRATE SHIP THE FEROSHUS MAGGOT

⚓ SKILLS INCLUDE ⚓

Head-butting
Eye-gouging
Pipe-smoking

Approach with extreme caution

Mabel wrapped her arms round his grubby fleece and gave him a great big hug. 'What are you doing here, Pelf?'

Pelf smiled at her. His tobacco-stained teeth glinted yellow in the lamplight.

'Well, it's like this, snuglet.' He nodded to a pair of large muscular dogs in sailor hats sitting at the bar and dropped his voice to a conspiratorial whisper. 'The Alsatian Navy has been cracking down on us pirates recently, so I came to the **NOO WORLD** to lie low for a while. I've bought myself a river boat and –'

He stopped suddenly and looked nervously at Carruthers.

'Did you say "us pirates"?' asked the badger suspiciously.

Pelf blew out a smoke ring that sank guiltily to the floor.

'Pirates? No! I can't stand those types, with their **fighting** and **swearing**. Not to mention habits as revolting as a communal plate of peanuts on a plague ship.' He sucked on his foul-smelling pipe and spat on the table.

'Pirates? Disgusting!'

Their conversation was interrupted by the sound of mocking laughter.

Mabel turned to see an immaculately dressed fox sitting at the bar. In his left paw he held a silver-topped cane; and in his right, a delicately balanced cocktail glass.

'Really, Speke! You're a long way from St Crispin's! And what a curious company of oiks you're assembling!'

Speke stood up proudly. '**Scapegrace!** I say, Scapegrace. Join us for a cup of tea?'

Scapegrace laughed again, revealing large sharp teeth. He twiddled his whiskers into a point. 'I'm afraid I'm rather busy planning an expedition, Timmy, old chap. Best you get on with your silly little tea party on your own!' He laughed again.

There was an embarrassed silence.

Speke sat down. 'He's awfully funny, isn't he?' he muttered. 'Same old Scapegrace. Always larking around.'

Mabel leant over the table. 'So who's this Scapegrace?'

Carruthers laughed bitterly. 'Sir Gideon Scapegrace is a fraud and a fool.'

Speke looked up. 'I say, Carruthers. That's *awfully* strong.' He smiled sadly at Mabel.

'We schooled together, Scapegrace and I.
At **ST CRISPIN'S SCHOOL FOR THE
EXCEEDINGLY RICH**.'

He glanced shyly across the room at
Scapegrace, who was now deep in conversation
with a bull terrier.

'Very popular chap: head boy and all that.
School captain. He took me under his wing, so to
speak. Let me clean his cricket boots, run errands
for him, tidy his rooms . . .'

Carruthers huffed. 'He treated you like a
servant, Timothy. Still does. It makes my blood
boil the way he talks to you. He's nothing more
than a **bully**.'

Speke frowned. 'I think Carruthers might be
a little envious, Mabel. Scapegrace is the world's
most celebrated explorer and author. His real-life
accounts of adventure and outrageous daring are –'

'Fanciful to say the least,' interrupted the
badger again. 'I doubt the rotter has even

been to Alsatia, let alone tightroped across the Schildkrote Falls.'

'I say, Carruthers. That is a serious accusation. You call the chap a liar? How dare you! Why, it was only last month that he told me that story in person. And very convincing it was too!' Speke sighed. 'His romancing of the archduke's daughter; his escape from the mountain gulag; his defeat, in hand-to-hand combat, of a twenty-strong Alsatian border patrol . . .'

Carruthers looked at his friend in alarm. 'You met him last month?'

Speke nodded. 'Yes. At my club. What of it?'

'Did you tell him about our expedition?'

'Of course not. You swore me to secrecy, remember? And an otter's word is as good as . . .' Speke paused. 'Well, naturally I mentioned the giant stash of ◆D◆◆I◆◆A◆◆M◆◆O◆◆N◆◆D◆◆S◆.'

'YOU DID WHAT?!'

Speke tapped his shiny black nose

conspiratorially. 'It's OK. I didn't say anything else. I was quite cryptic.' He chuckled to himself. 'I just mentioned that you and I were planning an exotic holiday together. To the **FORBIDDEN CITY**!'

Carruthers's face turned an angry red. 'Really, Speke! You are quite **intolerably** stupid!'

Pelf blew a cloud of toxic smog from his pipe and looked down at Mabel.

'It seems we're now in a race to the **FORBIDDEN CITY**, snuglet . . . against the great Scapegrace!'

'Erm, Pelf,' said Mabel, pointing at the two muscular Alsatians studying a WANTED poster hanging on the wall. 'Why do they keep looking round at you?'

Pelf coughed nervously. 'I think it's time we be leaving,' he said, pocketing the bag of coins and turning to Carruthers. 'Meet us at the jetty in one hour and we'll be getting underway.'

Together they stood up and began to walk to the exit, only to find the bull terrier blocking their way. On his head sat a smart bowler hat, and in his hand he held a short and dangerous-looking cosh.

From the bar came the sound of Scapegrace's laugh. He saluted them with his cocktail. 'Oh, Speke, I'd like you to meet my manservant, **WELLBECK**.'

The bull terrier snarled menacingly.

'If I were you lot, I'd get on the first boat home.' He looked at his cosh, then meaningfully at Carruthers. 'We wouldn't want any of you to meet with an **unfortunate accident** somewhere deep in the jungle, would we?'

He tipped his hat, bowed slightly and stepped out of their way.

Mabel and her new friends left the bar with the braying laughter of Scapegrace ringing in their ears.

Wait!

We're not ready for the next chapter yet!

Those impatient scuttlebugs who have already moved on to the next scene will have to miss out. Sometimes in stories such as this it pays to linger a little longer. For it is in these bits – the leftovers of chapters – that we find the most interesting of scraps: the fatty rinds of story-bacon. So hold steady and listen.

Can you hear it?

No?

Exactly!

There it isn't again. A strange silence that cuts through the hubbub of the crowded bar. A silence

that creeps from the corner unnoticed. The sort
of silence that only comes from one creature . . .

And what is this creature? A loris, of course –
a *silent* loris. A silent loris with one paw
replaced by a doorknob. His whiskers
twitch. Some head fur that grows in the
wrong direction is anxiously straightened
with a licked paw. This is O m y n u s
H u s s h .

He blinks his saucery eyes.

Was it her? Was it really Mabel Jones?

Omynus Hussh frowns and thinks back to the
last time he saw her. The day he was shot.

Of course I remember it well. And you may
too, if you have read the first of Mabel's unlikely
adventures.

We were friends, her and I . . .

Yes, indeed, Omynus. Mabel and you were the bestest of best friends forever. For she saved you and you saved –

She shot me!

What?!

She shot me and lefts me for dead!

NO!

I hates her.

A cold finger of pain shoots through Omynus's body. His good paw reaches through his jerkin to stroke the scar where the bullet entered his body and – here's the science bit – spilt the internal juices that have clouded his memories.

We know that it was the villainous **Count Anselmo Klack** who fired the almost-fatal bullet that almost-fatal day. But for Omynus Hussh the last thing he remembers is the pain of the wound and the face of Mabel Jones.

Water rims his saucery eyes, and an angry tear drips down his furry face. His hand tightly grips a suspiciously child-sized sack.

We'll gets her. And when we gets her . . .

We'll kills her!

CHAPTER SEVEN
Old Friends

So, then, to the jetty on the banks of the **Great Murky River** where the moonlight *would* dance upon the dainty waves if the water wasn't scummed with the filth from the **CITY OF DREAMS**. A ragtag collection of creatures hurriedly loads a rusting boat with supplies. Speke, the otter, sits apart, though, his skilled paws sketching the scene for posterity.

Let us peek over his shoulder. His work is entitled THE DEPARTURE OF THE BROWN TROUT FOR THE UNKNOWN INTERIOR OF THE NOO WORLD, BY SIR TIMOTHY SPEKE.

And though 'drawing' has always struck me as a trade for those too weak to hump a barrel down a gangplank and too scaredy to cut an albatross from the ship's rigging in the middle of a winter storm, Speke's drawing is a splendid thing.

Let me describe it for you.

That figure there is Pelf, the captain of the BROWN TROUT. A wanted pirate turned steamboat master. His pipe produces more smoke than the engine that turns the small paddle wheel that powers the boat – a decrepit two-decked sternwheeler. Lifting that crate is Carruthers, the scientist. He's helped by Mabel Jones (we recognize her, of course, although Speke has taken a certain **artistic licence** with her hair, making it slightly blonder and curlier than it should be). And with that the crew is complete.

But no!
Who is this?

A fifth crewman! A smut- and grease-covered engine-boy, a hooman snuglet!

His head peeks from a hatch over the small space where the old engine sits under the deck. He holds a spanner triumphantly above his head, for the fault he was working on has been fixed, but what the artist has captured even more exquisitely is the look of surprise on his face as he notices the presence of . . .

'MABEL JONES?!'

And so we leave the picture to witness a soppy scene. The two snuglets are now hugging in an engine-greasy embrace.

Let me explain. The boy is **JARVIS**, an old friend of Mabel's from her previous adventure.

Mabel stepped back and looked Jarvis up and down. 'What are *you* doing here?'

Jarvis rolled his eyes. 'Oh, apparently I did **THE DEED** again.'

Ahh, that explains it. **THE DEED**, like the

foul creepers, is a way of opening a porthole
between this future world and the one that Mabel
and Jarvis know as their home.

But, before Jarvis could explain any further,
a shot rang out across the night, and a bullet
whizzed between their heads and smashed a
lantern on the bow of the BROWN TROUT.

Mabel whirled round. A group of about ten
assorted animals was approaching along the jetty.
In among the tapirs, boars and monkeys, Mabel
could see the unmistakable bowler-hatted form
of Scapegrace's manservant, Wellbeck, urging
the band of brigands into action. Speke, the only
expedition member not on board, was scooping
up his pencils in fright.

'Full steam ahead!'

cried Pelf, pushing hard on a lever. Thick black
smoke poured from the chimney and the paddle
wheel at the back of the boat spun into life.

But the BROWN TROUT did not move.

The boat was still moored to the jetty, its paddle wheel futilely frothing the grubby waters of the Great Murky River.

'THE ROPE!' cried Mabel. 'Untie the rope!'

Speke put down his easel and started to undo the rope. 'It's an awfully complicated knot!'

The ruffians were getting closer. A tapir dropped to its knee to fire another shot.

Still the knot refused to budge!

'I say! It's stuck!'

Pelf drew his cutlass, leant over the side of the boat and sliced through the rope with one swing. The boat shot into motion, lurching away from the jetty.

'Jump!' cried Mabel to Speke, who stood gaping on the bank.

JUMP!' cried the rest of the crew.

A bullet splintered into the jetty by his feet and woke Speke from his bogglement. Rocking back on his feet, he took a standing jump and . . .

. . . landed short of the boat by centimetres.

Just in time, Carruthers threw out his hand and hooked his friend by the collar. Mabel rushed to help, and together they dragged him from the river and deposited him in a damp heap on the deck.

Mabel glanced back as the BROWN TROUT ploughed up the river. Scapegrace's ruffians had been left behind, their rifles out of range.

Carruthers glared at Speke. 'I say, Timothy, you really must stay awake. This is an expedition into the unknown, not a Whitsun cricket match!'

Speke just looked glumly over the side of the boat as the jetty disappeared into the distance.

'I left my beautiful picture!' He dabbed a tear from his eye with a hanky. 'I hope whoever finds it appreciates it.'

Pelf struck a match and held it to the bowl of his pipe. 'Narrow escapes from certain death. Just like the old days, eh, Mabel?'

Mabel nodded happily. The wind blew in her face as she stood on the bow, and the spray from the paddle wheel misted over the deck. It had been a while since she had been on a pirate ship – and admittedly the BROWN TROUT was more of a *boat* than a ship, but still . . .

Pelf patted her on the shoulder kindly. 'We'll find yer sister, snuglet. I promise ye that.'

He coughed and spat a massive phlegmy lump into the Great Murky River.

Mabel reached for the jelly babies in her pyjama pocket. 'Would you like one?'

Pelf raised a wild and woolly eyebrow. 'Sweets, snuglet? Ye'd do well to give those up. They'll rot the teeth from yer mouth.'

He grimaced, showing his smoke-blackened gums and nicotine-stained teeth.

'But that reminds me. There's a treat I been a-keepin' for ye, snuglet.'

Pelf reached down to a small locker and pulled out a cloth bundle.

Mabel unwrapped it eagerly.

'My cutlass!'

She grinned and made a practice cut through the air.

'**AVAST!**' she cried, and laughed her most piratey laugh.

CHAPTER EIGHT
The Brown Trout

*T*he gentle splashing of the paddle
wheel beat a steady rhythm upon
the waters of the **Great Murky River**
as the **BROWN TROUT** chugged slowly
upstream. From her position on deck, Mabel
could make out the jungle quite clearly on
either side. And what a jungle it was: a dark
and impenetrable mass of vines, creepers
and trees. Who knew what dangers lurked
within?

One thing was for sure: somewhere, deep
in its dark heart, was her sister, Maggie Jones.

Slightly inconvenient and a little bit annoying, but
her sister all the same.

How will I ever find her?

It seemed so hopeless.

And Mabel was right to worry. The jungle
sprawled for hundreds of miles, unmapped and
wild. Few had ventured into its dark interior and,
of those who had, fewer still had ever returned.

What hope of finding Maggie Jones?

None, frankly. No hope at all.

Just thinking of Maggie, all alone in the jungle,
made Mabel's heart beat in her chest like it was
about to burst. She forced herself to swallow.

I must find her!

She felt a paw on her shoulder. It was
Carruthers.

He looked at her kindly. 'That's it, my girl.
Keep a stiff upper lip. We'll rescue your sister.'

He nodded at Speke, who was sketching the scene. 'Speke and I are experienced adventurers. It is surely no accident that our paths have crossed. For we alone know the secret location of the **FORBIDDEN CITY**.'

Pelf secured the **BROWN TROUT**'s helm and joined them on the deck.

'And now it's time to share the details, badger. For there can be no secrets among crewmates.'

Speke nodded. 'Spill the beans, old chap.'

Carruthers placed his monogrammed briefcase on the deck and popped the fasteners open.

As he removed a bundle of papers, the crew eagerly gathered round.

'Behold the documents that will guide us to the **FORBIDDEN CITY**, where all our dreams will come true!'

Pelf rubbed his hooves together in glee. 'Ah, treasure! I can smell it from here!'

Carruthers motioned for silence and handed

Mabel a scrap of paper: a single page of an ancient and faded magazine.

Mabel read it aloud.

FOR HER

Cut from the finest of

A symbol of your undying love.
How could she resist?

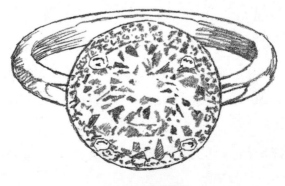

ONE OF THE THOUSANDS OF FINE PIECES
AVAILABLE AT TIFFANY AND Co.® OF NEW YORK.

She held the page up to show the others.

Below the writing was a photograph of a golden ring bearing a DIAMOND as big as a gorilla's fist.

Pelf sucked on his pipe thoughtfully. 'That sparkler must be worth a king's ransom! Think what a bloodthirsty pirate – I mean, think what an *honest-to-goodness river boatman* could achieve with such a fine fortune!'

Speke clapped his hands in excitement. 'I say! That's not all. Read the bottom bit, Mabel. The small print.'

Mabel squinted. Sure enough, partially faded but clear enough to read, at the bottom of the page was more . . .

ONE OF THE THOUSANDS OF FINE PIECES
AVAILABLE AT TIFFANY AND CO.® OF NEW YORK.

She scratched her head. 'Who's Tiffany?'

Jarvis looked at her curiously. '**Tiffany's**. It's a shop. It's *only* the biggest, most famous jewellery store in the world, silly.'

He smiled, wiping a greasy spanner on his overalls. 'In *our* world, I mean.'

Pelf chuckled. 'One of the *thousands* of pieces, eh? So tell me, badger. Where does I go to get me hooves on such fine lootery? Where is this **Noo York**?'

Carruthers pulled a map from the briefcase.

'This is the **NOO WORLD**!' He jabbed a finger
on the coastline.

'Here is the **CITY OF DREAMS**.

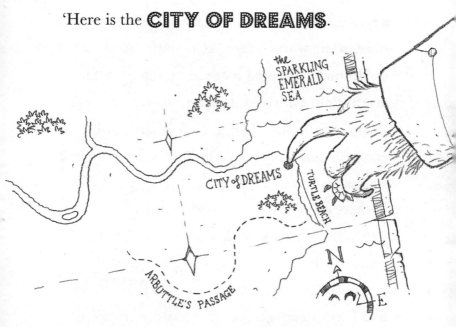

To the east: the *Sparkling Emerald Sea*.
To the west, north and south: the **unknown**!'
He paused . . .

for dramatic effect.

'Natives of this dark and sinister land speak of the **FORBIDDEN CITY**. A mysterious place that lies deep in the jungle.' He marked an X on the map. 'Here is its rumoured location. And *this* is the Great Murky River . . .'

His finger traced a snaking line that ran across the map from the **CITY OF DREAMS**. It continued its path even when the line on the map stopped.

'According to local legend, the river runs south of the **FORBIDDEN CITY**, then bends northward, taking us within a day's trek of its location. It is the only way to the **FORBIDDEN CITY**. Although no creature has ever made it there and back.'

Pelf blew a wisp of smoke that curled nervously behind his head. 'Maybe something to do with the evil Witch Queen who lives there?'

'Witch Queen, indeed. Poppycock!' Carruthers cleared his throat, then continued. 'I believe this city to be built on the ancient remains of the hooman settlement once known as **Noo York**.'

'But why do you think that?' asked Jarvis, looking at Mabel. 'In our time, **New York** is a port city – on the coast. On this map, it's right in the middle of the jungle. How is that possible?'

Carruthers smiled. 'Ah! Now that's where five years' hard work at MUNGO'S SCHOOL FOR TALENTED BADGERS, a scholarship to ST HILDA'S to study ancient history and a decade spent rifling through the dusty documents of the **CRUMBRIDGE LIBRARY** comes in handy.'

'Carruthers is awfully clever, isn't he?' whispered Speke to Mabel. 'Such humble beginnings too.'

Carruthers glared at his friend. 'If you'll let me finish, Speke.'

The badger pulled another map from his briefcase. 'This is a chart I've copied from the **CRUMBRIDGE LIBRARY OF ANTIQUARIAN MAPS**. They wouldn't let me borrow the original because . . . erm . . .'

Speke adjusted his monocle and sighed. 'Not the overdue fine, Carruthers! I could've lent you the money. You shouldn't be so proud!'

The white stripe on Carruthers's face bristled and beneath his fur Mabel could see him flush angrily.

'The reason why isn't important. It is enough that this drawn map is identical to the ancient map in the library.'

Mabel looked at it. 'It's a map of the **USA**!'

Jarvis nodded and pointed to a red dot.

'And there's **New York**!'

Carruthers smiled proudly. Carefully he placed the map of America over the map of the **NOO WORLD** and slowly began to move it around, muttering to himself.

'Now when we line up the mountain ridges

here . . . and these rivers there . . . Spin this round
to account for the rising and rotating of this
continental plate here . . . and the lowering and
crumbling of this plate there . . .'

Speke looked at Mabel. 'It's all just *science* to
me! I don't understand any of it!'

'There!' Carruthers stood up, beaming. 'It
matches.'

He held up the overlaid maps to the light so
they could see both as one.

The crew gasped.

The position of **New York** was directly
over the X Carruthers had marked to indicate the
location of the **FORBIDDEN CITY**.

Pelf laughed and blew a triumphant smoke
ring. 'And so we heads to the **FORBIDDEN CITY**
to pick up the biggest, sparkliest haul of loot that
ever there was! And rescue the sister of Mabel
Jones too,' he added guiltily. 'Full steam ahead!'

And with Pelf's command there was a loud
bang, a terrible grinding sound and a worrying
clank. The **BROWN TROUT**'s paddle wheel
ground to a halt, jammed by a bicycle that had
just at that second fallen from the sky.

'Awfully sorry, Timothy, old chap,' came a voice
from above. 'Seem to have dropped my bicycle
on your rusty little boat! I hope no one was hurt!
Haw haw!'

The crew of the **BROWN TROUT** looked up.

Just visible through the thick mist that shrouded
the jungle, a leering face could be seen looking

over the edge of a wicker basket suspended beneath a hot-air balloon.

'Scapegrace!'

cried Mabel.

The balloon was now rising steadily, and soon it – and the sound of Scapegrace's braying laugh – disappeared into the fog.

Jarvis looked at the jammed paddle wheel. 'It's not *too* bad. I expect we'll be able to start again in a couple of hours or so.'

Carruthers shook his fist at the sky. 'And in that time Scapegrace gets ever closer to the prize . . .

Our prize! The bounderous brigand! His
behaviour is most unappealing!'

Speke adjusted his monocle. 'I'm sure it was
an accident, Carruthers. Scapegrace wouldn't
deliberately try to leave us stranded in the jungle.
That would be poor form from a fox of such high
reputation . . .'

Carruthers glared at Speke, his bushy
eyebrows bristling. 'I must tell you that I hold
you **personally** responsible for this situation,
Timothy.'

'I say, Carruthers! How perfectly horrid of
you!'

And with that the two friends stormed to either
end of the boat, leaving Pelf, Jarvis and Mabel to
sort out the mess.

CHAPTER NINE
A Poisonous Silence

*T*wo days had passed since the argument between Carruthers and Speke, and not a single friendly word had been exchanged between them.

The BROWN TROUT paddled steadily along the river, never pausing. During the day, Carruthers kept his nose in the air, scouring the sky for signs of his rival, Scapegrace. At night, Mabel, Jarvis and Pelf took turns steering the boat carefully along the winding and twisting river. It was narrower now, and care had to be taken to avoid perils that lay in their path: sandbanks, drifting logs and, once, the remains of another similar craft, its rusting skeleton the only remnant of a previous failed expedition.

As the sun set on the jungle, it triggered a change of shift for the animals that lurked within its leafy realm. Gone was the birdsong and the constant **chirrup** of insects. The distant chatter of unseen creatures in the treetops faded away too. These sounds were replaced by the rustling of small mammals in the undergrowth, the low **GROWLS** of nocturnal predators, and the whispered chittering of large bats that swooped overhead.

But tonight was different.

Tonight was silent.

A strange kind of silence.

a suspicious silence.

Mabel Jones leant over the rail and watched as the jungle passed by. Pelf was at the helm, and Mabel planned to wander over later, in the hope he might share some stories of his time at sea. But for now she was content to breathe the cool night air and appreciate the rare silence that emanated from the mysterious jungle . . .

. . . totally unaware that the source of the silence was, at that very moment, sliding out of its nearby canoe and hollow-reed-snorkelling through some tropical weeds towards the boat on which she stood . . .

. . . planting its nimble toes on the hull of the BROWN TROUT . . .

. . . heaving its damp and hairy body silently on board, smothering the drips from its fur before they could drop upon the deck . . .

III

. . . and sliding up behind young, innocent, back-turned Mabel Jones, clutching a suspiciously child-sized sack in its one good hand.

We know now, of course, who this creature is. For, wherever there is a suspicious silence, there is usually the lurking of a silent loris intent on the foul deed of **CHILD SNATCHING**!

Omynus Hussh steps closer. His eyes narrow.

She was my friend!

His whiskers twitch.

She betrayed me!

He blinks nervously, angry tears forming in his large and saucery eyes.

I HATES her!

The sack is ready, the moment ripe, and . . .

. . . at that instant the clouds part and a lucky slice of moonlight falls upon his hand.

His *missing* hand.

His useless, *stupid* doorknob hand.

Omynus Hussh pauses. Last time he bagged Mabel Jones, he lost a front paw to her venomous bite, and now he has just the one left.

I's quite fond of my lonely handy!

The sack is rolled up and a new, more sinister plan is hatched. The good hand creeps up beside the leg of Mabel Jones, slender fingers questing for a pyjama pocket. Long, nimble digits slither inside, where a paper bag of jelly babies is located. The bag is removed without a single rustle. A jelly baby is plucked from its papery crib and its icing sugar sucked silently off.

WHAT TREACHERY IS THIS?!

Omynus Hussh pulls a small packet from his pocket.

A packet marked **POISON**!

It contains a fine white powder in which the sucked sweet is dropped and rolled until it is covered with a gentle dusting of death.

Then, finally, the sweet is replaced in the paper bag and the paper bag is replaced in Mabel's pocket and the loris returns silently to the shadows.

Hiding.

Watching.

Waiting.

CHAPTER TEN
The Journal of
Sir Timothy Speke

Tuesday, the 28th day of August: Day 7

A week ago, the sun shone off the Sparkling
Emerald Sea and the waves glimmered like a
thousand stars. It reminded me of Veronica's
eyes, and how they twinkled when she laughed
at my latest poem — an odd reaction to such
intense poetry of heartache and love, but she
has always been an enigmatic sort.

I remember that evening so well. As I declaimed my verses beneath her balcony, she laughed – then asked me to leave. The words I had spoken must have moved her so much she couldn't listen any more. It filled my heart with joy to know that she felt the same way as I do.

Tonight, though, I find myself in less beautiful surroundings. The vessel we've chartered to take us up the Great Murky River is an ugly tub. Carruthers, God bless him, remains his usual curmudgeonly and controlling self, but has at least allowed me some responsibilities – namely, being in charge of the supplies. It's good to know that we won't run short of damson jam in the jungle, even if it does mean the mosquito nets and hunting rifles had to be left behind to make space.

Talking of Carruthers, it has come to my attention that he is also in love with Veronica. He has not told me as much, but I can see it in his squinty badger eyes. The poor fellow doesn't know what's hit him, for love can't be quantified or studied like the scientific rot he is always waffling on about. Love is best left to the artists and poets of the world. People like myself . . .

I am a passionate otter, and I feel my heart must surely burst if I do not tell Veronica again that I love her.

I love her! I love her! I love her!

If Carruthers and I complete our mission and find the treasure of the Forbidden City, then surely I could treat her to the life she deserves.

CHAPTER ELEVEN
Captured

Days passed. The river grew narrower and progress was slow. Supplies were running out. And now the engine had spluttered to a halt.

Again!

Mabel sighed impatiently. Her sister was lost, somewhere in that dark and tangled jungle. Mabel could still hear Mr Habib's voice:

Your sister is in great danger . . .

She swallowed. Poor Maggie. She was only a baby. It wasn't her fault she couldn't rescue herself.

What was that?

A movement in the bushes! A shadow in the undergrowth!

The rest of the crew had picked up on Mabel's sudden alertness. Now they all stared at the bank.

Nothing.

It was **probably nothing.**

It was almost **certainly nothing.**

Definitely nothing.
Thank goodness!

Funny how the jungle plays tricks with your mind!

Jarvis's head appeared from the engine room.

He wiped sweat from his brow, leaving behind a greasy black streak. 'It's all fixed.'

The crew sighed in relief. The expedition could continue.

'I for one will be glad to get off this accursed sandbar,' said Pelf, opening the window of his cabin and spitting into the water.

A second arrow hit the cabin wall where Pelf's head would have been if the first arrow hadn't struck him in the chest, knocking him from his feet.

More arrows **thudded** into the boat! The crew dived for cover.

All was quiet, except for a soft moaning.

Mabel peeked out from behind a crate. 'Pelf? Pelf?'

The old goat let out another agonized groan.

'Pelf? Are you OK?'

'This is the end. I can hardly bear it . . .'

Jarvis looked up from behind a crate. 'Hang on, Pelf!' he cried. 'I'm coming to get you.'

Another batch of arrows thudded into the boat, forcing him to duck down again.

Carruthers pulled one from the deck and looked at it closely. '**The jungle egret!** See the elaborate feathering on this projectile? It's a classic example!'

There were more moans from the cabin:

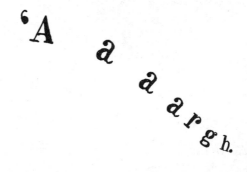

'I fear the worst . . .
All is lost!'

Carruthers looked at Mabel, his striped brow furrowed with concern. 'The jungle egrets are skilled bowmen. And these arrows are capable of delivering a fatal wound . . .' His voice tailed off.

Mabel pressed herself low to the deck and began to commando-crawl towards the cabin.

Pelf was lying on his back, the shaft of an arrow sticking from his fleece. Mabel raised herself to her knees and leant over her dear friend. 'Pelf?'

The old goat blinked at her and forced a grin. 'I fear it be a worst-case scenario, sweet snuglet.'

'Please,' she wept. 'Please don't die. Not you, Pelf!'

Pelf blinked. 'Die, snuglet?' he said. 'Why would I be a-dying?'

'The arrow!' Mabel pointed to the arrow sticking out of his chest.

'Oh, that!' He winced. 'It's true. The arrow has struck my most vital spot. Fatal damage has occurred . . .'

Pelf groaned and sat up. The arrow hung loosely, its point buried deep within his grubby fleece. Grabbing the shaft, he pulled it out, revealing the ripped bag of tobacco that had taken the full force of the blow.

'Ruined! That's the finest **WALRUS SHAG TOBACCO**.'

Mabel sighed with relief. 'It saved your life, Pelf!'

'And they say smoking is bad for yer health!' Pelf chuckled. Then he stopped chuckling. 'It looks as though we may be in some strife.'

He nodded towards the entrance of the cabin.

Two largish pear-shaped birds stood in the doorway, their tiny wings holding small bows, ready to unleash the poisoned arrows pointing directly at Mabel and Pelf.

Outside, Mabel could hear the voices of Carruthers and Speke protesting as more of the birds wrapped them in coarse jungle rope.

The BROWN TROUT had fallen – and her brave crew of adventurers was in grave trouble!

CHAPTER TWELVE
Skoo Cossin

*P*ull these ferns across your body.

Weave that jungle grass into your hair.

Now smear this mud across your face, for it will disguise your curious soapy scent.

Good work.

(I think it was mud anyway.)

Watch now from our hide in the undergrowth as we observe that curious creature of the forest floor, the **jungle egret**: a flightless and bottom-heavy bird. A plate from the unfinished work **ARBUTTLE'S BESTIARY** is included below for your reference. See figures 1a, a full-sized portrait, and 1b and 1c, diagrams of their means of stealthy attack. Ignore the splattered blood on the next page, for that is where they found poor Arbuttle halfway through his sketching. The unlucky fellow is buried around here somewhere.

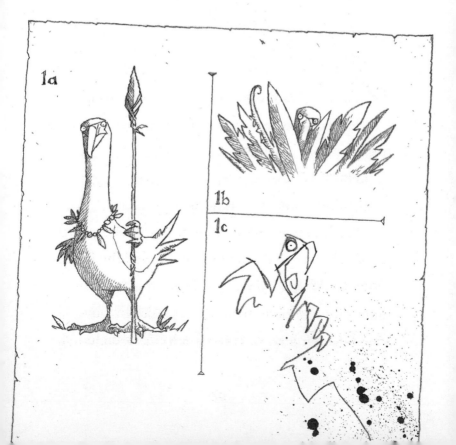

Stay silent and watch the egrets pass in single file. The captive crew are tightly bound and trussed to poles, which the egrets hoist upon their shoulders. An uncomfortable journey that can only get worse upon arrival, for who dares guess the motives of these mysterious jungle creatures!

After a long and winding trek through the undergrowth, the crew of the BROWN TROUT were unceremoniously bundled to the ground in

the middle of a village of neatly woven grass
huts. Egret villagers gathered round, occasionally
jabbing at them with **sharp sticks** and
quacking excitedly.

A bird with an elaborate ornamental feathered
headpiece stepped forward. He quacked at the
crowd and they fell into a hushed silence.

'I say, who is this chap, Carruthers?' asked Speke.

Carruthers rolled over. 'For goodness' sake,
Speke. It's the chief of the village. Keep quiet.
We don't want to do anything to makes this grave
situation worse. Look at that!'

In the corner of the clearing, atop a pile of logs, was a battered bowler hat. And sticking through the bowler hat was an arrow!

'Wellbeck's hat!' gasped Speke. 'Do you think he's . . .' He turned his head away from the sight. 'How horrid!'

Carruthers nodded grimly. 'It looks as if Scapegrace and Wellbeck were here before us – and in similar trouble. That is why we must be *very* cautious indeed.'

'Yes, of course, Carruthers. I'll handle this. Needs some of my trademark charm, what?'

Speke cleared his throat and addressed the chief. 'Hello, old chap! Awfully sorry to bother you. Would you mind *terribly* pointing us in the direction of the **FORBIDDEN CITY**?'

Immediately the tribe broke into angry quacking. Bows were drawn, sticks pointed and feet stamped on the forest floor.

The chief lifted a wing above his head and once

again the tribe fell silent as some of the birds that
had attacked the boat came forward and untied
Mabel and Jarvis, separating them from the others.

The stripe on Carruthers's nose bristled
with anger. 'What are you doing with them? As
expedition leader, I demand you unhand my –

OUCH!'

A nearby bird had jabbed his right buttock
with a sharp stick.

'You swine! You've drawn blood!'

Speke, enraged at the treatment of his friend,
struggled against the ropes that bound him. 'Foul!
Unsportsmanlike behaviour! No ball! Shame!'

The chief signalled again and Speke,
Carruthers and Pelf were lifted up and carried
away into a hut.

Jarvis looked at Mabel with wide eyes. 'I'm
definitely not frightened, but what do you think

they want with us?' he whispered, in a voice that sounded a little bit frightened.

'I'm sure it's just a misunderstanding,' whispered Mabel in a voice that sounded anything *but* sure.

She felt his hand slip into hers. Sometimes it was easy to forget that Jarvis, as well as being a skilled engineer, was just a little boy.

But then the strangest thing happened. As their hands touched, the villagers gasped and threw themselves on the ground. Even the chief stared at them with wide eyes, then bent down on one knee.

He cleared his throat with a short quack and, with obvious effort, began to speak.

'Skoo Cossin?' he said.

Mabel blinked. She wasn't sure quite how to reply.

'Skoo Corsing?' tried the chief again.

Mabel and Jarvis looked at each other in confusion.

The chief frowned.

'Skoolk Rossing?'

Finally, with a frustrated
flap of his wings, he turned
and quacked at the crowd.
An elderly bird stepped forward,
carrying a heavy bundle. He placed it on the
ground and gently removed its ceremonial blanket
of woven leaves.

Mabel and Jarvis stared at it. It was an ancient
metal sign, rusted and discoloured, and clearly
of great value to this strange tribe of birds. But,
despite its obvious age, despite the ravages of
centuries gone by, Mabel and Jarvis recognized
it immediately. There were similar signs in their
own time. In fact, they saw one every weekday.
Two children, shown as black silhouettes: one girl
and one boy, holding hands above the words . . .

'SCHOOL CROSSING!' they exclaimed
together.

The crowd broke into a celebratory chorus of quacks. Once again the chief signalled for quiet.

'You. Skool Crossing.' He pointed at Mabel and Jarvis, then at the sign.

Ah!

Mabel looked at the sign. It was clear what was going on now. Mabel and Jarvis looked like the children on the sign! Especially since they were holding hands.

Holding hands!

They were still holding hands.

Mabel quickly let go of Jarvis's hand. Who knew where it had been? Mabel wiped her palm on her pyjama leg.

The chief pointed at them. 'You. Go. Skool.'

Mabel and Jarvis nodded. It seemed they were getting somewhere at last. They did indeed go to school.

The chief smiled. 'You. Go. Skool. You. Save. Tribe. Kill. Scuttling. Death.'

Mabel looked at Jarvis. **Scuttling Death?**

Mabel didn't know who or what Scuttling Death was, but it certainly didn't sound very pleasant. They certainly didn't study Scuttling Death Killing at *her* school. Maybe they followed a different syllabus here?

She smiled politely. 'Erm, well, if you don't mind I think we'd better –'

The chief interrupted with a quack. **'You. Kill. Scuttling. Death . . .'** His face darkened to an angry scowl.

'Or.

    We.

        Kill.

            Your.

                Friends!'

CHAPTER THIRTEEN
Maryvale High

Have you ever wound your way on foot through the hot and steaming jungle? Its heat sucks the air from your lungs and its moisture weighs you down. Each step you take feels like ten. Is that vine a **venomous snake**? Is that non-venomous snake a **poisoned vine**? Yes, every shady glade can conceal a parade of potential predators poised to pounce. And that useful stick you are using to fend off thorny vines **– why, that is no stick!**

That is the dreaded ᕱᗝᑎᕮ ᗰᗩᑎTIᔕ: a well-camouflaged stick *insect* that has probably already laid its eggs beneath your fingernails. Make sure you scrub them well this evening or the eggs will hatch and microscopic larvae will burrow into your finger bones to feed on the richly nutritious marrow.

Mabel Jones and Jarvis picked their way carefully through the undergrowth. Their guide, a fierce-looking egret with nimble feet, looked nervously at the sky. In the jungle, with twilight comes a welcome drop in temperature and an unwelcome rise in crepuscular carnivores.*

He speared a large spider from the path with his sharpened stick.

'Dinner,' he quacked.

---

* Footnotes are for the swots, teachers and other bottom-feeders that skim the seabeds of pages looking for the pointless plankton of knowledge. I suggest you stick to the story in future.

Then he broke off
one of its legs, took a
bite and offered the
rest to Jarvis.

'I'm all right,
actually,' said
Jarvis politely.

The egret
shrugged, then
carefully wrapped the spider
in a large leaf and tucked it
safely into his bag.

'Pudding,' he explained.

The path wound its way up to the crest of a
hill. At the top, the jungle dropped away into a
vast valley that swept downward to disappear
into the evening mist. A distant hooting echoed
through the gloom.

Mabel paused for breath and adjusted her
backpack. They had been equipped with all the

essentials of a jungle expedition by the egrets: an oil lamp plundered from the BROWN TROUT, some strange medicinal herbs and, of course, a pair of ceremonial preserved kidneys taken from one of the egrets' previous captives.

She looked at Jarvis. 'Somewhere out there is the **FORBIDDEN CITY**,' she said.

Their jungle guide looked at her with frightened eyes. '**Shh**hh! FORBIDDEN CITY so forbidden it forbidden to say "**FORBIDDEN CITY**". Many egret lost to dark magic . . .' He looked around the jungle nervously. 'Enslaved by Witch Queen!'

Mabel gulped. 'I hope Maggie's OK.'

It was dark now. The egret stopped and held up a wing. They had come to a junction in the path.

'Which way do you think?' asked Mabel, idly scuffing her foot across a small pile of bones on the jungle floor.

A PILE OF BONES?!

She stepped backwards and knocked over another pile of bones.

ANOTHER PILE OF BONES?!

She bent down and picked up a small skull with a long thin beak. It was the remains of a jungle egret!

Jarvis shuddered. 'A victim of the Scuttling Death?'

Mabel nodded. 'The school must be here somewhere. At least we have our loyal guide to help us find it.'

She turned round to find that their loyal guide had vanished.

'Where did he go?' asked Jarvis.

Suddenly there was a strange creak . . .

Followed by an unusual groan . . .

And then, without any further warning . . .

THE GROUND **COLLAPSED** BENEATH MABEL'S FEET AND SHE WAS falling!

CHAPTER FOURTEEN
A Lovely Picnic in the Park

Mabel Jones was having a lovely picnic in the park near her house.

The whole family was there.

Mum, Dad, even Maggie.

'MABEL?'

Mum handed her an egg sandwich. 'There you go, love.'

'Thanks, Mum!'

She bit into the sandwich and chewed it thoughtfully.

It was nice to be home.

'MABEL?'

Someone was calling her. A voice from far away.

Go away! Let me have my picnic in peace.

She took another bite of her sandwich. But now it was different. There was something crunchy in the egg mayonnaise. A bit of shell maybe? She tried to spit it out but brittle fragments of the stuff seemed to have filled her mouth . . .

What's this I'm eating?

'MABEL, ARE YOU DOWN THERE?'

She carefully peeled back the top layer of bread and saw that the filling of her sandwich wasn't egg mayonnaise but actually the crushed beak of the poor jungle egret upon whose remains she had toppled.

She shuddered and looked up at her mum.

But her mum wasn't her mum any more.

Instead, beady eyes shone beneath the whispery eyebrows of Mr Habib!

He was reaching across the picnic blanket to touch her nose . . .

'Your sister is in great danger . . .'

A fragment of beak choked her. And still Mr Habib's paw came closer.

'The ultimate sacrifice must be made . . .'

She clawed at her throat, desperate for air.

'MABEL, PLEEEASE ANSWER ME!'

And then she woke.

All around her was dark.

She groaned. Her whole body ached. She put her hand to her head.

Blood!

It's just a scratch! she told herself sternly. Pull yourself together, Mabel Jones.

She looked around slowly.

She was lying on the remains of the table that had broken her fall. An old-looking piece of paper lay across her chest. Mabel peered at it.

MARYVALE HIGH SCHOOL, said the heading. **ADVANCED CALCULUS**.

'An exam paper,' she said thoughtfully.

Some metres directly above her, the dim moonlight shone through a hole in the ceiling. Jarvis's head was peering through, his eyes squinting into the darkness.

'Mabel, are you OK?'

'I'm fine,' she called. 'I think I've found the school!'

Getting on her hands and knees, she scrabbled around. Eventually her hand found the familiar-feeling straps of her backpack.

Carefully she opened the bag and pulled out the oil lamp. It was a bit fiddly but she managed to light it. Mabel sighed with relief. Somehow everything felt better now she could see.

Well. She might have thought that. But some things are best left unseen, for nothing could have prepared Mabel for the sight that was revealed in the flickering light of the flame . . .

CHAPTER FIFTEEN
A Sight Best Left Unseen

I'm often asked, 'Of all the many onions available to the hobby pickler, which variety would you recommend and why?' Of course, the answer is always –

I beg your pardon?

Oh, I'm sorry, that's actually a line from my other book. You're reading this one, aren't you?

Where was I?

Ah yes. Mabel Jones and a sight best left unseen!

In the flickering of the lamplight, among the

dancing shadows cast by the flame, was a sight that sent cold grey fear crawling over her skin like a troop of chilled maggots looking for a warm spot in which to pupate.

SKELETONS!

Hooman skeletons!

Sitting one per desk, and dressed in the tattered remains of their clothes: a cap here, a pair of shoes there, baseball jackets and sparkly hairbands. Mabel gasped.

Students!

All were facing the front, where a larger skeleton sat at a larger desk, with a coffee mug and a magazine. Its elbow was on the desk, a thumb lodged into the hole where its nose would once have been – as if frozen in the motion of picking a bogey in the trademark and duplicitous style of an adult.

Coffee . . .

Nose-picking . . .

A teacher!

Mabel's eyes explored the large room. The flickering light of the lamp revealed the half-collapsed remains of an ancient school gymnasium, the sports equipment safely stored and the room lined with row upon row of examination desks. The roots of large trees punctured the ceiling and vines hung from the rafters. Over time, the school had become buried by the advancing jungle, seemingly lost forever!

The students of Maryvale High School had never finished their exam. The teacher never got to finish his coffee.

Here they had sat for years upon years. Something had happened to them.

Something had happened a *long* time ago.

Jarvis's voice plucked Mabel from her daydreaming.

'Do you want me to try to pull you back up?'

'Yes, please!'

Mabel sighed with relief. It was good having back-up. Even if he was only a little boy.

Jarvis smiled. 'I've found a vine. I'll lower it down. You can tie the vine round your waist and –'

Suddenly there was a loud scuttling sound . . .

Then a muffled cry . . .

Then . . .

The vine fell to the floor beside Mabel.

'Jarvis?' she cried.

'JARVIS?'

No answer.

Jarvis had disappeared.

Dead, I reckon.

Another victim of the Scuttling Death – the beast that lurked around and deep within this ancient school.

A moment's silence, please, for in these circumstances I believe it is best to assume the worst and give up all hope . . .

CHAPTER SIXTEEN
A Moment's Silence

What's that noise?

Do you mind? Have you no respect?

Oh! It's Mabel Jones.

She runs through the gymnasium, frantically searching for a way out!

A way to get to Jarvis!

She still has hope.

She is not the sort to give up on one of her friends.

Not like you.

Shame on you!

If there's one thing I always say, it's:

'NEVER GIVE UP.'

It's a motto I like to live by.

CHAPTER SEVENTEEN
The Principal

*M*abel stood before a small room. It was closed off from the gym by a heavy metal grate that took all her strength to lift. It was a store cupboard. Neatly packed sports equipment lined the walls. No way out here! Stepping back, she let the grate fall closed with a loud bang that echoed around the gymnasium.

Next she found a door. She tried pushing it but it was stuck fast. The partial collapse of the gymnasium had wedged it firmly in place, but Mabel found a rotten section and kicked a hole in it. Squeezing through on her hands and knees, she found herself in a long corridor with doors on either side. Lockers lined the walls. The place was full of dust.

Suddenly there was a scuttling noise to her left. She jumped and spun round, drawing her cutlass.

There was nothing there.

Then the noise came again. This time from behind a door marked PRINCIPAL'S OFFICE.

Cautiously she approached.

'Jarvis?' she whispered. '*Jarvis . . . ?*'

A sound broke the silence. A strange gargling voice came from inside the room, speaking dreadful words:

'I can smell blooooooooood!'

Mabel stopped. She put a hand to the cut on her head.

'Where's my friend?' she demanded.

The voice from inside the room spoke again.

'He's getting ready for dinner.'

'Jarvis? Are you in there?'

'Won't you join us?'

The door swung open. A draught of air rushed out and extinguished the lantern.

Mabel Jones was

plunged

into complete darkness!

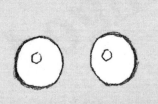

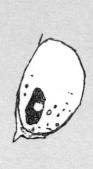

Mabel jumped backwards into the corridor.
She was just in time. The Scuttling Death
swooped its head towards her, its mandibles
snapping empty air.

Mabel held her cutlass out and roared:

'MY NAME IS
MABEL JONES,
AND I'M NOT
SCARED
OF ANYTHING!'

The Scuttling Death laughed a wet laugh.
Drool hung from its jaws, dangling in large drops
that swung below its face.

The monster swooped again.

Mabel twisted out of the path of its mandibles,
but she was too slow to avoid the beast altogether

and her cutlass was knocked to the floor.

Then it struck again. Its head crashed against her side and sent her spinning down the corridor where she landed, dazed, at the foot of a trophy cabinet. A large wooden shield covered in the names of a succession of spelling-bee winners fell next to her.

The Scuttling Death lunged forward. Mabel held the shield out in front of her. The beast's jaws bounced off and it shrieked in pain.

There was a stand-off.

They glared at each other, both breathing heavily.

Then the monster attacked again. Once more the shield took the full force, but this time it spun from Mabel's grasp and she went skidding back down the corridor towards the gym.

The Scuttling Death shook its dazed head.

'I'll get you, little juicy one.'

Quickly Mabel squeezed back through the hole in the gymnasium door. The giant millipede came after her, its mandibles snapping empty air once more, as she pulled her trailing foot through the hole.

Safe.

For the moment.

But there was no other way out and Jarvis was still in the creature's wicked clutches.

Mabel shuddered.

Jarvis was going to be eaten!

It was the kind of moment when you need a really good idea.

And then she had one.

CHAPTER EIGHTEEN
The Exam Room

THUDDDD!

The door of the gymnasium shook with the impact from the Scuttling Death's head.

'I can smell you. I can smell your blood!' it gurgled through the hole.

THUDDDD!

The door shook again.

THUDDDD!

With the third thud, the door gave way. Rubble fell from the ceiling and bounced off the giant millipede's armoured head.

The Scuttling Death looked around. It was a creature of the dark, dank underground. A creature that normally surfaced only on the blackest nights, when its hunger for the jungle egret overwhelmed the urge to stay safe in its subterranean lair.

Its eyesight was poor. It lifted its head and sniffed the air. **'I can smell you, little one.'**

It scuttled closer and then sniffed again.

Sure enough, the smell of Mabel Jones's bloodstained pyjamas drifted faintly through the air.

'Closer and closer I come . . .'

His blurry vision fixed upon a Mabel Jones-sized object.

'It smells like you . . .'

It stalked closer to the store cupboard where poor frightened Mabel Jones sat rigid, frozen stiff with terror.

The Scuttling Death blinked.

'It looks like you . . .'

And, with those words, the creature pounced.

Mabel didn't have time to move. She didn't even seem to try. The monstrous mandibles mashed down on her head and . . .

CRUNCH!

The Scuttling Death looked confused. Mabel Jones was not the juicy snack it was expecting. This was a dusty husk: a snuglet-pasty without its filling – a low-fat alternative to a real child.

What could have happened?

The monster's eye fell upon a stick. A lacrosse stick – strangely not dusty, as though it had recently been taken from storage – propping up the heavy metal grate of the store cupboard.

The *real* Mabel Jones stood up from a desk nearby, wearing the baseball jacket that had once belonged to the skeleton she had dressed in her pyjamas and positioned in the store cupboard. In her hand she held an American football.

I only get one chance!

And she threw it, knocking over the lacrosse stick and releasing the heavy metal grate, which fell with a large

bang

and severed the head of
the Scuttling Death with
such force that it flew from
its body across the room,
bounced off a wall and
landed firmly wedged in a
basketball hoop.

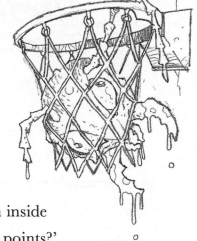

A weak voice came from inside
the store cupboard. 'Three points?'

Mabel raced across and heaved open the grate.

Jarvis lay within, still trapped inside the
cocoony sac of the Scuttling Death.

Mabel tugged the sac free and tore at the sticky
membrane until it split.

Jarvis fell out, gasping for air. 'I don't feel too
good, Mabel,' he whimpered.

'You'll be all right,' said Mabel, scrubbing him
clean with her jacket sleeve. 'Now, help me get my
pyjamas back. We've got a baby to rescue!'

CHAPTER NINETEEN
The Journal of
Sir Timothy Speke (cont.)

Friday, the 31st day of August: Day 10

I write this safely aboard the Brown Trout, chugging once more up the Great Murky River, deep into the heart of the jungle. Today the hooman children returned, their mission accomplished and, in his gratitude, the chief has set us free. But with our freedom came a grave warning – the Forbidden City is an evil place. The proud tribe of jungle egrets has lost many of its members to the ruins. They believe the rumours that the city is ruled by an evil Witch Queen, even if Carruthers dismisses them as superstitious rot.

Today the rain pours down, and we huddle in the small space under cover. All apart from the captain, Pelf, who stands at the helm and keeps us clear of sandbanks. A tricky task, for the rain creates a steamy mist in this hot jungle habitat.

And there is more worrying news: Carruthers is in a bad state. His right bottom cheek, punctured by the spear of a jungle egret, has swollen to twice its normal size. I fear the wound is infected from an embedded splinter, for he lies in a fever. He sweats and rolls in his bunk, calling Veronica's name. The poor chap must be delirious. He seems to think there has been some kind of arrangement of marriage between them, for he cries: 'I do! Veronica, I do!'

I should go to his side. As I write, the remaining crew gather to discuss the best course of action . . .

'Is it even **possible** to amputate a bottom?' asked
Mabel Jones curiously.

Pelf shrugged. ''Tis our only hope. If that
splinter don't come out it will be the death of him.'

He wiped his cutlass on his yellow-stained
fleece. 'That should be clean enough!'

Carruthers gritted his teeth through the pain.
'I'm not letting any of you filthy brigands near my
nether regions!' He looked up at Speke. 'Timothy,
despite your many failings at least you have good
hygiene. You must follow my instructions.'

Speke nodded bravely. 'I'll make you proud,
Carruthers.'

'Firstly, fetch the box of **emergency
equipment** . . .'

Speke reached into a crate and pulled out
a small tin box. He looked at Mabel eagerly. 'I
packed it myself! Only the best equipment for –'

Carruthers interrupted, his voice weak with
pain. 'Make haste! For this splinter **must** be

removed. Speke, you have to open the wound and extract it. It is the source of an *intense* discomfort.'

Speke scrabbled in the first-aid box and held up a multi-bladed pocketknife.

'You did purchase the Explorer edition, didn't you?' asked Carruthers. 'The one with the knife, built-in compass *and* tweezers?'

Speke shook his head. 'I decided against that version, Carruthers.'

The others looked at him as he started opening the pocketknife's multiple blades.

'Ladies and gentlemen, I present to you the very latest in outdoor accessories: **The Wilkins Picnicman™!**'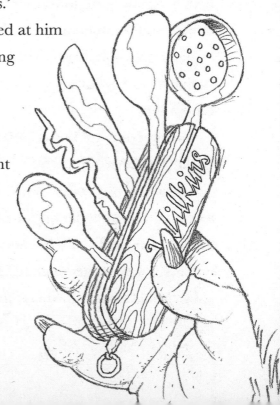

He smiled proudly, holding up a rounded flat blade not unlike a toddler's butter knife.

Pelf grunted and blew out a cloud of toxic smoke. 'That couldn't cut through the hide of a mouldering sardine!'

Speke looked a little upset. 'It's a pâté blade,' he explained. 'It's meant for *spreading* not cutting.'

He opened another, similar tool. 'And this one is for your coarser condiments. Your piccalillies, shredded marmalades, onion chutneys, et cetera.'

With a flourish, he demonstrated the rest of the implements. 'Corkscrew, sugar tongs, tea strainer, napkin ring . . . All in one handy accessory!'

Carruthers's eyes boggled. 'Is that it? Is that **all** our emergency equipment?'

'Of course not,' cried Speke indignantly. 'We also have instant coffee! Just in case we have guests from . . . er . . . of . . .' He looked awkwardly at Pelf. 'Of a less refined nature!'

Carruthers jumped to his feet. 'Why, I'll

throttle you, Timothy! You've brought nothing
to this expedition but whimsy and picnic
accessories!'

'I-I say, Carruthers,' stammered the otter, his
voice breaking with emotion. 'The scones! What
about my mother's scones? You said they were
delicious!'

'THEY. WERE. DRY!'

cried Carruthers, clenching his
swollen right buttock in rage. Then
he turned on his heel and
limped to the bow of
the boat, where he
proceeded to
glare moodily
at the river
ahead.

   Speke sat
dejectedly on the

stern. 'I am such a fool. I'll never amount to
anything,' he sobbed. 'Oh, Veronica, how could
I ever believe you might choose me?'

Mabel Jones patted Speke on the shoulder.
'There, there,' she said. 'We'll think of
something.'

Then she paused, bent down and picked
something up from the deck.

'Look – it's the splinter. It's come out!'

Carruthers turned. 'Why, it must have popped
loose when I was clenching my buttocks with
rage . . . Speke, old fellow, can you forgive my
temper?'

Speke nodded sulkily. Then he looked at
Mabel.

'That badger wouldn't know a good scone if
you threw one at him!' he muttered.

CHAPTER TWENTY
The Last Known Whereabouts of Gideon Scapegrace

*P*erch on the branch of this tree that stretches over the tepid waters of the **Great Murky River**. Dangle your lower limbs if you must, but take care not to dip your toes beneath the surface. For this stretch of the river is home to numerous species of carnivorous fish that can strip a cow to its bones in under a minute, and to a particularly painful parasitic footworm.

Here they come!

You can hear the chugging of the BROWN TROUT long before it appears round the bend in the river. Its paddle wheel churns the water, and the river is narrow enough for the wake from the boat to gently lap the banks. Mabel Jones is at the helm and she carefully steers the BROWN TROUT upstream towards their destination.

His right buttock carefully bandaged, Carruthers studiously examines the map. They are nearing their goal.

THE FORBIDDEN CITY!

Mr Habib's words tug at Mabel's memory strings.

I see an ancient tower that grows from the black and burnt earth of a forbidden city . . .

She looked at the thick forest that lined the bank. They were so **close** to finding Maggie . . .

There was a movement on the shore.

A rabbit stood up, its head poking above the undergrowth, its nose twitching. It blinked and ducked behind a bush. Then it popped its head up again.

Mabel smiled and waved. 'Hello there!'

The rabbit waved back.

'Isaycouldyouhelpmedownfromhere?' it said.

Mabel cut the engine. 'I beg your pardon?'

'Isaycouldyouhelpmedownfromhere?' repeated the rabbit.

Mabel scrunched her nose up in the way people do when they are confused.

The rabbit spoke again.

'Isaycouldyouhelpmedownfromhere?'

It beckoned to her.

Mabel let the BROWN TROUT drift towards the bank. Jumping overboard into the shallows, she moored the boat to a tree stump.

The rabbit disappeared into the undergrowth.

'Where did it go?'

Pelf blew out a thick cloud of smoke. 'There!' The rabbit beckoned again.

'Isaycouldyouhelpmedownfromhere?' it said.

The crew of the BROWN TROUT carefully disembarked and followed the rabbit along a narrow path that weaved through the thick undergrowth. Eventually they came to a small clearing. Many other rabbits were sitting around. They hopped over to inspect the strange visitors.

'Isaycouldyouhelpmedownfromhere?' they chorused.

'It's awfully perplexing, Carruthers,' said Speke. 'Why *do* they keep saying that?'

Carruthers scratched his head. 'More to the point, where did they learn that particular phrase?'

Mabel looked up. 'I think I know,' she said. 'And I think it's bad news . . .'

Carruthers, Speke, Pelf and Jarvis slowly followed her gaze upward.

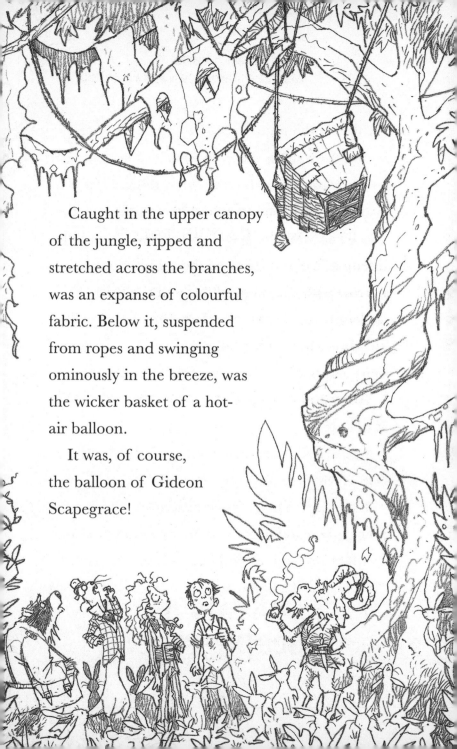

Caught in the upper canopy of the jungle, ripped and stretched across the branches, was an expanse of colourful fabric. Below it, suspended from ropes and swinging ominously in the breeze, was the wicker basket of a hot-air balloon.

It was, of course, the balloon of Gideon Scapegrace!

It took the best part of a day for Pelf to construct a winch from ropes foraged from the hold of the BROWN TROUT. From a nearby tree, he hoisted Mabel into the upper canopy.

Once level with the wicker basket, she grabbed the rim and pulled herself in. The basket lurched under her added weight. Mabel looked up at the ropes nervously. The basket had been hanging for some time and the ropes had started to fray.

Carruthers's voice called from below. 'Is he still in there?'

Mabel grimaced and shouted back, 'Yes! He's here all right.'

For opposite her, still safely strapped in its seat belt, was the immaculately dressed body of a fox.

It was
Sir Gideon
Scapegrace!

The Last Known Whereabouts
of Gideon Scapegrace

In his hand he held a tightly rolled piece of paper. Gritting her teeth, Mabel Jones slowly peeled back the death-stiffened paw from its treasure.

It was a note.

CHAPTER TWENTY-ONE
The Last Words of Gideon Scapegrace

Please forward to my publishers.

This is the last chapter in the autobiography of me, the great Gideon Scapegrace, celebrated balloonist, acclaimed daredevil, beloved explorer, etc. etc. [Fill in the usual details here please, Susan.]

It was a dark and stormy night but I was sure that, with the help of my trusty hot-air balloon, the Narcissus, I could find the Forbidden City. It was to be my finest hour since the liberation of the Duchess of Kataslavia. [Has she dropped her court case, Susan? Awful shrieking creature. How was I to know she WANTED to get married to that squinty-eyed archduke?]

My journey had been spiced with the usual peppering of danger. The balloon, punctured by the arrows of the savage jungle egret, swooped low over the trees. My biceps bulged as I unloaded the ballast of my precious bicycle [and Wellbeck, my co-pilot – please inform his mother, Susan, and remove any mention of him from previous chapters]. Fate was on my side as the Narcissus gained enough height to keep from snagging on the branches of the jungle canopy.

At times it seemed as though the jungle was infinite, a never-ending sprawl of mysterious tropical vegetation, but then, finally, I sighted it: the Forbidden City. It was barely a mile away! I could see the shape of a looming tower shrouded in mist. A tower so tall it touched the blackening clouds that swirled portentously [Is this the right word, Susan?] overhead.

But, just as my prize seemed to be within my grasp, a sudden tornado burst from the city. In an instant, it took hold of the Narcissus, blowing us back into the jungle. The balloon, already damaged by the arrows of the jungle egrets, crash-landed in the upper branches of this infernal tree, where I sit and write this final chapter.

And here I remain, dangling high above the forest floor, my only hope of rescue, the tribe of rabbits that live in these parts. Unfortunately they seem unable either to reach me or understand my instructions. They just repeat my requests for help.

So ends the thrilling life of Gideon Scapegrace. And I leave it with this final warning to those who would seek the Forbidden City:

Turn back! Stay away from this accursed place! For if it is inaccessible to the great Scapegrace, then it is inaccessible to all!

Mabel Jones looked up from the note.

The **FORBIDDEN CITY** was close!

She peered into the distance. Through the hazy mist she could see something. A grey shape rising above the treetops.

A TOWER?!

She looked at Scapegrace's remains.

We have to succeed!

We have to rescue Maggie!

Oh, what's that?

Mabel squinted at a small grey moth that crawled from beneath Scapegrace's top hat.

Pelf called across from a nearby tree. 'Careful, Mabel. That looks like the **tropical vine moth**! Many a sailing vessel has been left ropeless by the ravenous creature after laying anchor in a jungle bay. Its caterpillar eats through the toughest of ropes. My old crewmate **Claude Surepaws**, a rigger, fell from a snapped rope eaten away by the worm of the vine moth!' He clapped his hooves together to indicate the flattening effect of such a fall.

'**SPLAT!** Flatter than a flatfish pancake!'

Mabel Jones shuddered at the imagined end of Claude Surepaws.

Then another moth flew past.

Then another.

She suddenly felt very nervous indeed.

Then...
TWANGG!

One of the three ropes suspending the basket from the canopy snapped. Mabel was flung to one side and out of the basket. Desperately she scrabbled for a grip on something, anything!

Until her hand grabbed the arm of Gideon Scapegrace.

He jerked forward, his seat belt holding fast.

MABEL JONES WAS HANGING SIXTY METRES ABOVE THE JUNGLE FLOOR, HER FINGERS GRIPPING THE WRIST OF A RECENTLY DECEASED HOT-AIR-BALLOONING FOX!

'I say, Mabel,' cried Speke. 'That looks awfully dangerous!'

Mabel stared.

Her arm was starting to ache.

I . . .

can feel . . .

my fingers . . .

slipping . . .

And, with a shriek of purest fright, Mabel Jones let go.

CHAPTER TWENTY-TWO
Plummet to the Death

*P*oor plummeting, tumbling-to-her-death Mabel Jones.

Falling . . .

Falling . . .

Falling . . .

THWACK!

The impact from the **rare blue buzzard** felt like being struck by a car.

It took the wind from Mabel Jones's lungs and shook her eyeballs nearly clear of their sockets. But, however much it hurt, it was infinitely better than the impact from the ground that would have certainly killed her if she had reached it.

Sharp talons gripped Mabel's shoulders. She stretched up and felt soft feathers and scaly legs, and she held on tightly. The buzzard had enough strength in its wings to hover for a few seconds.

Then
   they
      began
        to
          fall
            again.

Tumbling through the air in a mass of flapping feathers and struggling snuglet, they came to the ground in a crash of twigs and leaves.

Mabel Jones blinked.
She was alive.

Shaking her hair free of leaves, she turned to face her rescuer. The buzzard looked at her with expressionless beady eyes. It was the same blue buzzard that Mabel had saved from roasting all those days ago in the squalid shack of Mr Habib!

Pelf drew his pistol. 'Careful, Mabel, stay still – ye be not safe yet! That overgrown herring gull probably thinks ye be its dinner.'

'Wait!' cried Mabel. 'Don't hurt him!'

She smiled and scratched the buzzard's head.

'Squawk?' she said.

The buzzard looked at her and smiled back.

'You're welcome, Mabel Jones,' it said. Then, stretching its wings, it took a lolloping run and, with a few loud flaps, soared into the sky.

Mabel watched the majestic creature disappear into the jungle mist.

'Well, it was certainly worth rescuing you!' she said to herself. 'And talking of rescuing . . .'

There was somewhere she had to be.

CHAPTER TWENTY-THREE
The Forbidden City

*L*et me tell you a story. The story of a city –
maybe the greatest city **ever**.

A city built on an island, where the mouth of
a broad river met the mighty ocean. A city built
by giant machines. Huge towers of brick, glass,
steel and concrete rose from the ground, winched
together, piece by piece, until the city was almost
as high as it was wide. Bridges spanned the river
and the city grew bigger still, stretching as far as
the eye could see. Hoomans filled the streets, all

'How's it goin'?' and 'Have a nice day!' and
Toot toot toot!

Until one day the city fell silent.

The echoes of their great machines, the hubbub of the busy streets and the growling of their cars settled like dust upon the ground. Not a honking horn was heard, nor a policeman's whistle, nor the laughter of a snuglet. Just the sound of the wind blowing off the water, rattling through the empty avenues and blowing the litter of the last day of hoomanity along the gutters, where it gathered in drifts of filth.

Yes, dear reader, all things come to an end . . . Even the hooman race.

The city became an empty and lifeless wreck, like the shell of a giant African land snail, eaten from the inside out by the larval stages of a parasitic wasp. And for years it remained that way, while the plants reclaimed their places.

Creeping vines climbed the walls, their hairy tendrils crumbling the buildings brick by brick. **Trees** broke through the roads, their roots causing the pavements to undulate and crack. **Moss** covered the old abandoned machines and lichen hung from the street lights like the beards of sun-wizened castaways.

The land beneath the city changed too. Springs sprang up (as is their habit) and turned streets to streams. The rivers that flowed on either side of the city dried up and, as the vast continents of which the world is made shifted and groaned, the sea retreated, until a thick tropical jungle enveloped the city entirely.

Just one creature remained – a relic from the city's past.

A creature of unspeakable evil.

A creature who enslaved the animals of the jungle and brought them to the city and set them to work.

Cutting,
hacking,
burning.

Lifting,
patching,
repairing.

Rebuilding a great tower on the orders of the Witch Queen herself.

Look! A movement in the undergrowth: beneath the ferns, in the broken remains of an ancient building. Mabel Jones and her brave expedition of adventurers. The first creatures from the OLD WORLD ever to set foot in the **FORBIDDEN CITY**. Picking their way through the undergrowth and scrambling over the rubble.

Follow Mabel's gaze. For before her she sees the tower, rising tall among the ruins. A building half of brick and steel, half of wood and vines: a ramshackle collection of the ancient and the new. Into the sky it climbs, from a patch of scorched earth where the jungle has been burnt away, leaving only the blackened skeletons of the trees that once grew lushly around its feet.

Look closely at Mabel now. Silently she mouths the words she heard all those days ago from the lips of Mr Habib:

I see an ancient tower that grows from the black and burnt earth . . .

Mabel has reached the **FORBIDDEN CITY**.

Mabel has reached **New York**.

The sound of grunting startled her from her thoughts. Through the undergrowth Mabel caught sight of an unhappy group of egret slaves approaching, pulling wooden carts of rock and stone.

One of the egrets looked at her blankly. It was different from the ones in the jungle village –

thinner, with bald patches where feathers had fallen from its coat. Mabel started as she looked into its cold, dead eyes. It blinked and, for a moment, a sparkle of life returned to its face. A look of fear.

Pure fear.

'Witch Queen . . . sees all,' it said. 'You must . . . escape!'

And then the sparkle dimmed and the blankness returned.

Mabel felt Jarvis's hand creep into hers.

'I don't like this, Mabel. I don't like this one bit!'

CHAPTER TWENTY-FOUR
Tiffany's

Crawl with me now into this leafy tunnel that forces a path beneath the thick, thorny undergrowth. We come to an ancient wall, once solid concrete, now crumbled rubble. Scramble over its remains and sit in the shade of this large flower that emits an overpowering, choking smell of rotten meat. Hopefully it will hide your scent from the many wild predators that hunt near these ruins. For we now sit on the only remaining floor of a once-colossal building. A square archway survives where a grand doorway stood. And through that doorway now steps a ragtag bunch of tired and weary adventurers.

Carruthers fumbled in his briefcase, then held aloft a scrap of paper.

'Scholars of ancient civilizations at the **UNIVERSITY OF CRUMBRIDGE** believe that this map is a plan of the **FORBIDDEN CITY** at the height of its success.'

The others gathered round his tatty and aged document.

'If we triangulate the position of that tower over there –' he motioned to the great tower – 'with the same tower on the map, then we should be able to locate the place known as **Tiffany's**. We need the compass to work out which way is north. Speke?'

Speke held up the wrong kind of compass. 'What sort of circle would you like me to draw?'

Mabel coughed politely.

'I know where **Tiffany's** is.'

Carruthers squinted at the map. 'I think we need to head down this avenue. It seems to be a raging torrent now, though. Maybe it's actually that way . . .'

Jarvis frowned. 'I think it might be *that* way!'

He pointed to a broken road leading into dark, overgrown jungle.

Mabel coughed again, a bit less politely. 'I know where **Tiffany's** is.'

Carruthers looked up crossly.

Then they all gasped.

For Mabel was holding something in her hand. Something that streamed from her fingers like a tiny waterfall frozen in time: the sparkliest, shiniest, ◆D◆◆A◆M◆O◆N◆D◆◆I◆E◆S◆T◆ necklace any of them had ever seen.

Pelf sighed and toxic pipe-smoke curled out from his nose holes.

'All those years spent sailing the seven seas in

search of treasure, and what have I got for it?
Nothing but a warrant for my arrest, a sea-mite-
infested fleece and a handful of shattered dreams.
But now . . .' Pelf slapped Carruthers on the
back. 'Why, there be enough sparklers in this here
necklace for me to buy a ship . . . A proper ship!
A PIRATE SHIP.'

Speke looked at him, boggle-eyed. 'Do you mean
to say that you *are* a pirate?! I'd never have guessed!'

'Well, I can't say that the **ROYAL INSTITUTE OF
EXPLORERS** will approve of the treasure being
used for piratical purposes,' said Carruthers, 'but
they might turn a blind eye once I present them
with a diamond for their museum.'

Jarvis had wandered off a little. 'I think you'll
be buying more than one pirate ship, Pelf!'

The others turned to look at him.

Mabel laughed, for she had never seen such
a sight. Jarvis stood there, arms outstretched,
swathed in diamonds. Diamond bracelets, diamond

necklaces and a diamond tiara.
Handfuls of diamond rings
dripped through
his fingers. His eyes
were wide open in
delight.

'They're all over
the place!' he said,
giggling, and he picked up
another necklace.

Pelf took out a large sack and began filling it
with the diamonds.

Carruthers paused and frowned. 'Where is it?
The big ring! The one in the picture.' He pulled
out the old scrap of magazine and read aloud.
'*For her. Cut from the finest of diamonds. A symbol of
your undying love. How could she resist?*'

Mabel pointed to a sign that hung crooked
on a wall above some steps leading downward to
darkness.

VAULT

'Maybe in the vault?'

Pelf nodded. 'Aye, the greatest treasures are *always* kept **underground**. Them's the rules!'

Lighting a torch, the explorers slowly descended the stairs, which opened out on to a small room with a large circular metal door at one end.

Pelf sucked on his pipe. 'A safe!' he exclaimed. 'And a big one at that. Oh, for a brass cannon and some ARMOUR-PIERCING CANNONBALLS.'

Mabel popped a jelly baby into her mouth. Her second-to-last one.

Somewhere in the darkness of the shadowy vault, a silent assassin twisted his doorknob in excitement.

Mabel swallowed the jelly baby and . . .

and . . .

and . . .

Nothing happened.

Somewhere in the darkness of the shadowy vault, the silent assassin rolled his saucery eyes.

Meanwhile, Carruthers had been inspecting the safe door.

'A door this thick would require a tremendous amount of pressure to break. I'm not even sure a cannonball would do it . . . I wonder if there's some way to override the locking mechanism.'

Mabel coughed. 'Maybe it isn't –'

'Science won't help us now,' interrupted Pelf. 'I say we come back with a hundred sticks of **dynamite**.'

Mabel coughed again. 'We haven't even tried –'

'Sir, the careful application of scientific methodology always triumphs over brute force,' snapped Carruthers. 'What we need to do is . . .'

Mabel didn't bother interrupting again. She

just pulled the safe door and it swung silently and smoothly open.

She smiled. 'It wasn't even locked,' she said.

Then she stopped smiling.

A hooman skeleton sat on a chair in the corner of the safe. An ancient security guard's hat balanced on its skull.

In the middle of the room was a **plinth**.

And on the plinth was **a glass box**.

And in the glass box was **a ring**.

And on the ring was the . . .

LARGEST,

SHINIEST, SPARKLIEST

EVER.

AND I MEAN EVER!

Carruthers held aloft the ancient advert. 'It's
THE ring!'

Carruthers looked at Speke.

Speke looked at Carruthers.

Their eyes narrowed.

'For Veronica!' they cried in unison, racing into
the safe.

✳

Oh, !

Many a pirate or similar land-based varmint
has come a cropper due to the glittering stones
known as diamonds. Once you have seen one –
once you have *held* one, spinning it round in your
fingertips so its many facets catch and turn the
sunlight to rainbow – once you've seen it sparkle
like a star plucked from the night sky, then . . .

Well. No good comes from such things.

Carruthers and Speke raced towards the ring,

with Mabel, Jarvis and Pelf right behind them . . .

Cut from the finest of diamonds.

. . . their arms outstretched . . .

A symbol of your undying love.

. . . their jaws hanging open . . .

How could she resist?

No one could . . .

Apart from Omynus Hussh.

For misplaced hatred beats dumb greed in
the Top Trumps of emotion, and his thirst for
revenge on Mabel Jones outweighed his desire to
hold the diamond.

Just a single silent step into the light.

Just a tiny wicked glint in his saucery eye.

Just a little push!

And slowly, softly, silently the safe door
began to swing shut.

CHAPTER TWENTY-FIVE
The Dreaded Thunk

THUNK!

CHAPTER TWENTY-SIX
Ramifications of the Dreaded Thunk

*T*he sound echoed around the inside of the safe like the memory of a bad dream.

Mabel Jones and her companions were trapped! And this time there was no way out!

Mabel felt sick.

Then she had that *other* feeling. That feeling you get when you've done something wrong. Something *really* wrong. Like when you've forgotten someone's birthday, or broken their favourite toy. This feeling was a similar flavour to that feeling but much stronger. And it grabbed at her guts and it clawed at her throat, till finally it found its way to her mouth and burst out in a sound that was half cry, half sob.

'MAGGIE! I forgot about Maggie!'

Mabel clawed at the door, her bitten fingernails scrabbling at the cracks.

'We must get out!'

She punched the lock.

'We must,
we must!'

But it was no good.

The others watched her in silence for there was nothing that could be said.

They were trapped. Entombed forever. For the sake of a diamond.

Mabel Jones sat down and began to cry.

She cried for herself.

She cried for her mum and dad, who she might never see again.

And she cried for her sister, Maggie. Poor not-really-that-inconvenient, not-really-at-all-annoying Maggie Jones.

Then she stopped crying and began to think.

CHAPTER TWENTY-SEVEN
The Tower

*J*oin me on this elevated platform strung from
the bamboo scaffolding that climbs beside the
tower that grows from the burnt and blackened
jungle.

On the highest floor there is a single room,
enclosed with glass walls on all sides. We can
enjoy the panoramic view of the once-great city.
And what a view! The ruins of **New York** lie
all around, disappearing into the misty wet haze.

The room is bedecked with the finest
scavengings from the deserted city: *opulent*

furnishings from the best apartments, the *finest art* from the crumbled museums, and the worthiest of books from the city's libraries.

A choking, sickly-sweet smell hangs heavy in the air.

The odour of magic.

Dark magic.

This is the Witch Queen's boudoir.

Ferret yourself away in the folds of the glamorous ballgown that hangs from that hook over there: a dress made hundreds, maybe thousands, of years ago, found and claimed by the Witch Queen.

Nice, isn't it?

Breathe in its elegant perfume. Feel the fine fabric between your fingers. Place your face against the trimmings. It looks and feels as good as new!

You'd never guess it is riddled with an infestation of plague-bearing lice.

Or that the dress is to be worn for the foulest of foul deeds, an evil purpose beyond belief.

For this dress is to be worn tonight. At the ceremony where the Witch Queen finally sheds her dying and withered body and takes a new form: a **hooman form**.

Outside, the enslaved egret drummers drum a sacred beat. A storm has been summoned: see the black clouds spiral around the great tower like evil candyfloss.

The reconstruction of the tower is complete. Once again it reaches high into the clouds, ready to harness the power of the storm. Only one thing is missing: the hooman body itself – Mabel Jones.

F o o t s t e p s !

She approaches! The Witch Queen is upon you! Push yourself further into the folds of the gown, and listen to a soft yet cracking voice, like the sad melody of a recorder carved from the timbers of a hangman's rotten gibbet.

'The one called Mabel Jones is close . . .'

Hide silently beneath the fabric and pray. Pray to the gods of good fortune, the goddesses of fluke. Grip the lucky sausage of chance tightly *and* cross your fingers, for you must not be discovered.

Me?

Oh, I should be fine where I am. Luckily I popped off a few moments ago to find a bite to eat in preparation for the final chapters.

The Witch Queen speaks again.

'For years I have waited for this moment: for a hooman form to inhabit. And with that form I shall take my place in the hooman world, to live as she might have lived . . . Yes, thou art close. Thou art close indeed, Mabel Jones . . .'

She reaches out for the ballgown you have hidden yourself in. Dry, scaly hands brush down its fine

silken folds; sharp painted
nails miss your face by the
breadth of a mermaid's
chin-whisker.

Can you hear her fetid
breath wheeze through her
shrivelled lungs and rattle her
brittle ribs? Can you smell
the smell of death upon her?

'It is time. Time to
summon the fury of the
spirits of the storm. Time
to harness their rage from
the angry clouds that gather
overhead. Time for the
demons who lurk deep within
the bowels of the earth to
rumble and shake the city,
for great power is needed
for the . . .

TRANSMOGRIFICATION OF MABEL JONES!'

The Witch Queen strikes her warped and
wicked staff upon the floor – and the city begins to

shake. . .

CHAPTER TWENTY-EIGHT
Bad News

*B*ack in the safe, there was nothing to do but wait.

Mabel took the paper bag of jelly babies out of her pocket.

One left.

Her last sweet ever.

She looked around the reinforced room.

Carruthers was staring at the diamond ring, wondering how to get it out of its glass box.

Speke sat in the corner, completing the final entry in his diary.

Jarvis was studying the lock, trying to see if there was any way he could pick it.

Pelf tugged at his beard and frowned. 'There's not much air down here, snuglet. If we don't get out soon . . .' He lit his pipe and blew out a thick cloud of toxic smoke. 'What good are diamonds to a dead pirate?'

Speke smiled sadly. 'I have but one regret, Mabel, and that is Veronica. For I fear that she will wait a lifetime for me to return.'

Mabel grimaced. Being trapped in an inescapable doom for the sake of something sparkly seemed like a lot of effort just to impress a girl.

'You'll understand love one day, Mabel,' sighed Speke, patting her on the head. 'But, until you do, allow me to share my feelings in the form of a poem . . .'

Mabel cringed in embarrassment as Speke began to read from his notebook.

'*The memory of thy furry face fills me with feelings*
Deep as the flavour of a fine Stilton cheese . . .'

Mabel frowned. Speke was right. She didn't understand. No one was worth this amount of struggle and pain.

Then she remembered why she was here.

'*Without thee I am like that cucumberless sandwich,*
My crust removed but left rejected . . .'

Maggie.
Maggie was worth it.

'*You are the jam in my Victoria sponge,*
To moisten an otherwise joyless existence.'

So, Mabel thought, maybe she *did* understand what love was, after all. She loved Maggie. And she would do *anything* to save her.

'For what point is a picnic alone, Veronica?
What point is a life without . . . love?'

Speke's voice faded into a sad silence. He
wiped a tear from his furry face.

A short sob escaped from his mouth. 'Oh,
Veronica! Forget your darling Timothy. He has
been lost, tragically young *and* before really getting
the recognition for his art that he truly deserved.
I implore you, cast off your mourning and find
another (albeit less artistic and poetic) suitor. For I
am **dead**!'

He sighed. 'If only there were a way to get her
a message – a letter for example. Anything.'

The word 'letter' bounced around Mabel's
head for a moment. Then it settled in the part of
the brain where forgotten memories are stored,
and dislodged a thought.

A letter?

Oh goodness! The letters!

She reached into her pyjamas, pulled out the letters she had pocketed all those days ago in the Hotel Paradiso, and handed them to Speke.

'I forgot about these. They're addressed to you and Carruthers.'

Speke gasped and pointed to an embossed wax seal bearing an elaborate coat of arms. 'By crikey! It's Veronica's seal!'

He held the envelope to his nose and took a deep breath. 'That scent! Oh the sweet fragrance of POLECAT MUSK. I'd recognize it anywhere.'

Taking out the pâté blade on his **Wilkins Picnicman™**, he neatly opened the envelope and slid out a pink card. He read it to himself, smiling at first, but then slowly his brow creased and his lip began to quiver.

Mabel tensed. 'What is it? Bad news?'

'Oh, Mabel. It is the worst news. I feel my heart might break!'

He held the card out for Mabel to see.

**SIR HEATHCOAT AND
LADY MILLICENT POLECAT**

invite you

to the marriage of
their beautiful daughter

MISS VERONICA POLECAT

to

SIR CATCHPOLE CRIBBINS, MP

The Church of the Benevolent Stoat

Crumbridge

DRESS CODE: ARISTOCRATIC

RSVP

Speke looked at Mabel, tears rolling down his
face.

'How . . . could . . . she?' He screwed up the
invitation. 'And to Cribbins of all people! I knew
he was a rotten egg.' He sighed. 'Awfully rich,
though . . .'

Carruthers looked up from the diamond.
'What's that about boring old Cribbins?'

Quickly Speke hid the letters.

'Oh, nothing. Just remembering our days
together back at school. I think the bad air is
bringing on delusions,' he lied.

Carruthers nodded sagely. 'Indeed. It is a grave
situation we find ourselves in. With every minute
that passes, the air gets ever thinner.'

'Aye. If only we could do something that would
make it last longer,' mused Pelf, and he pulled
out his reserve pipe and lit that in preparation for
when his main pipe went out. He put down the
sack full of diamonds and sat on it, dejectedly.

Speke looked at Mabel, holding a paw to his mouth to stop a sob escaping. 'You must promise not to tell Carruthers, Mabel. It would break him. It is too much for his heart. He has never loved and lost before . . .'

Mabel nodded. She thought of Maggie, lost somewhere in the city. A prisoner of whoever had snatched her from their bedroom. Lost forever, unless a miracle happened.

And, with that thought ringing in her head, there was an almighty rumble and the room began to

shake . . .

CHAPTER TWENTY-NINE
Earthquake

*M*abel was **thrown** to one side of the room.

Then she was **thrown** to the other side.

Then they were all **hurled** into one of the corners.

Then all was still.

Mabel looked at Pelf. 'What was that?'

'An **earthquake**,' he muttered, staring up at a giant crack that had appeared in the ceiling. 'It's going to bring the roof down upon our heads, snuglet!'

Carruthers bristled. 'Nonsense! If you consider the density of the building material against the magnitude of the tremors, factoring in the torsional rigidity provided by the vault's arched structure, it would take a far larger earthquake than that to –'

There was a **loud snapping** sound and the grinding of twisting metal. A vast and cavernous crack danced across the floor, mere centimetres from his feet. Pelf jumped up as his sack of diamonds toppled backwards into the hole.

'My loot!' he cried.

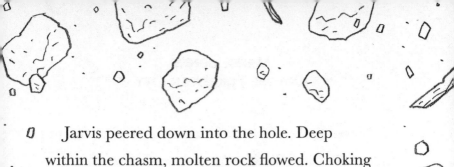

Jarvis peered down into the hole. Deep within the chasm, molten rock flowed. Choking sulphurous smoke curled up into the room.

'It's like the inside of a **volcano** down there!' he said.

There was another rumble and vast lumps of masonry started to fall from the ceiling.

'I say,' said Speke. 'Look at this!'

The glass case had been smashed by a lump of falling rock, and the giant ring was at his feet. He stooped and picked it up. 'It's a smasher! Awfully heavy, though!'

Pelf sucked on his pipe. 'Still more than enough treasure for all of us!'

Mabel sighed. She had more important things on her mind. She looked across at the other side of the room.

The force of the earthquake had buckled the circular safe door. A small gap had appeared at the bottom.

'If we can get across the chasm, then we might make be able to make it out. This earthquake could *save* us!'

There was another rumble.

The safe door creaked and groaned under the pressure.

More rocks fell from the ceiling.

The chasm grew ever wider.

Mabel looked at the others and they nodded in agreement.

'Jump!'

And together the five of them ran for the crack.

Mabel landed first, and the momentum took
her to the door. Turning round, she saw Pelf,
Jarvis and Carruthers leap and clear the chasm.

Only Speke remained on the other side,
clutching the giant diamond ring in both hands.

'It's no good!' he cried. 'I can't do it. It's too far.'

Mabel looked nervously at the ceiling. The whole place was about to collapse.

Carruthers stepped forward calmly. 'Listen, Timothy. You *can* do it. I know you can.'

'You think so, Carruthers? I mean, you *really* think so?'

The badger smiled. 'Of course, Timothy. I believe in you.' He turned to Mabel, Jarvis and Pelf. 'We *all* believe in you.'

Speke nodded. He twisted his monocle tightly into place, then, stepping back, he took a small run up and jumped . . .

. . . plunging, several metres short of the edge, into the

deep,

dark

chasm.

CHAPTER THIRTY
Within the Chasm

'SPEKE!!'

It was all Mabel could do to hold back Carruthers from jumping in after his friend.

As she peered into the chasm, a small tear fell from her eye, to sizzle and disappear into steam as it touched the molten lava that had engulfed Sir Timothy Speke.

Pelf joined them at the chasm's edge.

'Alas, 'tis a grisly end. And an unfair one at that. He was a fine artist, if ye like that kind of thing. Which I don't.'

He spat respectfully on the floor.

And a voice floated up from somewhere in the darkness of the chasm.

'I say, chaps, that's terribly kind. I'm blushing, I really am, but would one of you mind awfully lending me a hand?'

Then, as the sulphurous fumes parted, Mabel could see him. Clinging to the wall of the chasm by a single paw, the other clutching the

giant ◆D◆I◆A◆M◆O◆N◆D◆ ring.

Carruthers fell to his knees. 'Oh, Timmy! Timmy, you're alive! Hold on!'

'I'm awfully afraid I might have to let go,' replied Speke. 'This ring is frightfully

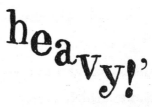

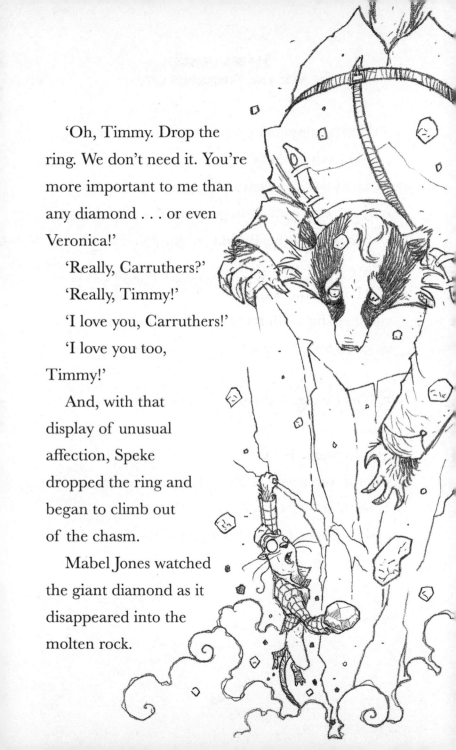

'Oh, Timmy. Drop the ring. We don't need it. You're more important to me than any diamond . . . or even Veronica!'

'Really, Carruthers?'

'Really, Timmy!'

'I love you, Carruthers!'

'I love you too, Timmy!'

And, with that display of unusual affection, Speke dropped the ring and began to climb out of the chasm.

Mabel Jones watched the giant diamond as it disappeared into the molten rock.

'I hate diamonds,' she said. 'They bring a whole lot of trouble.'

Pelf blew a sad smoke ring. 'They'd have bought me a whole lot of pirate ship too, though.'

Mabel looked around the room.

'It's about to collapse! Quick!'

They squeezed through the crack in the buckled safe door and ran up the stairs. Ducking and dodging falling chunks of masonry, they rushed out on to the pavement just as the ruined remains of the jewellery shop known once, long ago, as **Tiffany & Co.**, New York, disappeared forever into the huge hole that had appeared beneath it.

Mabel drew her cutlass and swiped it through the air. 'Now it's time to rescue Maggie!'

But, just as she was about to start wondering how *exactly* they would do that, she noticed a sound that wasn't coming from deep within the hole.

Not a rumble.

Not the hiss of broken building meets molten lava.

Just silence.

ɑ ꜱᴜꜱᴘɪᴄɪᴏᴜꜱ ꜱɪʟᴇɴᴄᴇ.

She peered over the edge of the hole, into the darkness.

A pair of saucery eyes blinked back at her.

'*Omynus?*'

The eyes scowled. 'Leave me. I don't needs help from a nasty snuglet. I *hates* you more than I hates . . . more than I hates . . . more than I hates the ache in my proper fingers on my proper handy that grips to this slippy rock.'

But Mabel didn't even hear his cruel words. She had already started to climb down into the hole.

'I'm coming to get you, Omynus!'

Rock by rock she climbed down. A crevice here, a narrow ledge there, a crumbling patch of loose earth –

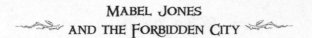
SHE'S LOST HER FOOTING!

SHE'S FOUND IT AGAIN!

I cannot watch.

Deeper down she climbed. Deeper into the bowels of the earth.

She could see him properly now, hanging from a jagged crag of rock, silhouetted by the burning lava that flowed beneath.

'Grab my hand. I'll pull you up.'

'Would do if I had a spare one! You bits it off, remember?'

He waved his doorknob at her angrily.

Mabel grabbed it in one hand and, with all her might, hauled the whining loris from his precarious outcrop to her slightly less precarious outcrop. And there they sat, panting with the exertion of the rescue.

Then, with a snarl, Omynus Hussh scurried up the side of the hole as fast as if it were the ship's rigging he had been raised on all those years ago aboard the **Feroshus Maggot**.

A minute later, Mabel reappeared at the top of the hole. There was no sign of Omynus.

'Where is he?' she asked. 'And how can he be here? He was dead. I listened to his chest – there was no heartbeat.'

Pelf puffed on his pipe. 'Aye, snuglet. But who knows how quietly beats the heart of a silent loris? He must have survived after all.'

'But why did he say he **hates** me?' pondered Mabel Jones. 'We have to find out.'

'There isn't time, Mabel,' replied Jarvis. 'You'll never find him if he doesn't want to be found. And Maggie still needs to be rescued.'

Mabel frowned. Jarvis was right. This was one mystery that would have to wait.

She looked around.

'Goodbye, Omynus,' she called. 'I miss you.'

Somewhere in the shadows, a silent figure squatted, watching as Mabel Jones and her friends headed deeper into the jungle.

Omynus Hussh scratched his head.

She saved me. Why?

And a familiar warm feeling crept up inside his gut, surprising his heart and triggering the true memories lurking deep within his brain.

The shiny gleam of a pistol . . . a finger on the trigger . . . a finger belonging to a fully grown hooman, not a tiny snuglet . . .

The Count!

Omynus Hussh started.

It was the Count that shots us, not Mabeljones! Mabeljones was my friend.

He blinked a happy tear from a saucery eye. 'She's *still* my friend!'

CHAPTER THIRTY-ONE
The Gathering

The storm has reached its height and darkness has enveloped the **FORBIDDEN CITY**. The streets are illuminated with the lit torches of thousands of jungle egret slaves, all trooping in silence to pay homage at the great tower – finally finished and ready to perform the task for which it was rebuilt: to harness the power of the storm in a ceremony of evil purpose. But we should be safe up here, high above the canopy in this ruined building that stands opposite the great tower.

Careful of that bird's nest!

The **FORBIDDEN CITY**, hidden so deep in the impenetrable jungle, is home to many rare species. It would be a shame to lose that lonesome fluffy chick over the edge – it is the last surviving offspring of some rare hummingbird, I'll warrant. Pass it over here. I shall store it safely.

Between these two slices of bread!

Delicious!

Before us stands the mighty tower. You may recognize it from your own time, or you may not. Around its base, the Witch Queen's enchanted slaves take their places for the final act.

All waiting for the Witch Queen to make her appearance.

Now scan the crowd. Mabel Jones should be there somewhere. Where can she be?

Mist starts to gather and a murmuring spreads through the gathered crowd.

'The Witch Queen is coming . . .'

'The Witch Queen is coming . . .'

'The Witch Queen is . . .

HERE!'

It was a blob, a shapeless lump, that crawled
from the grand doorway of the great tower.
A huddled figure swathed in a silken gown.
The crowd watched in silence as it began its
slow journey down the many steps towards the
clearing.

It was the Witch Queen.

And as she hobbled from the last step and
crawled across the ground, her fingernails digging
into the dirt, dragging her hindquarters behind
her, she laughed a dry laugh like the crumbling of
a bonemeal biscuit.

She stopped in the middle of the clearing and raised herself on her hind legs with the aid of her gnarled and crooked staff.

What kind of animal was she? For animal she certainly was, that was clear. Despite the blood-red lipstick, despite the painted nails, despite the freshly shaved fur, despite all her desperate efforts, she was no *true* hooman.

Her skin was wrinkled and pale, mottled with rusty spots and patches of fur in the places a razor could not reach. Her eyes were milky pools of pure evil. And her mouth? A lipstick-lined and puckered hole decorated with **rotten fangs**.

It is whispered that the Witch Queen had been alive before the city fell. Before the glass cracked and the bricks crumbled and the steel warped. But this cannot be true, for that would make her **thousands** of years old. Surely nothing can live that long?

Can it?

But, then, I know little of jungle magic or the old ways.

The dark ways.

The Witch Queen looked around the crowd, her blind eyes seeing all. Every single creature winced and cowered before her gaze.

She paused, took a long sniff and spoke in the soft croaking tones of a dying toad. 'She is here. The one called Mabel Jones is among us!'

She looked into the crowd once more.

'WHERE ARE YOU, MABEL JONES?'

And then she **howled**, a hideous shrieking

HOWL

that echoed through the city and over the jungle, and all who heard it – whether hooman or beast – shivered with fear.

The Witch Queen scratched her mottled skin, and flakes of it caught the breeze and drifted through the city like grey ash fluttering from a bonfire. She took a small and wriggling bundle from inside her gown and laid it gently upon the ground.

A hooman snuglet! A double-wrapped and swaddled little sleeping grublet! We are too far away to tell for certain it is Maggie Jones – for all hooman babies look alike – but surely it must be she!

Look!

A movement in the crowd: a nervous twitch. Did you see it? There, at the back!

IT'S MABEL JONES!

Held back by her loyal friend, Pelf.

'It's a trap, snuglet!' he whispers.

Mabel knows he is right. She pauses.

'Ye will not save her like this!'

He's right, Mabel. Hold steady, my dear. Hold steady.

But the Witch Queen's wickedness knows no bounds. She is not constrained by such things as rules, or manners, or lists of Top Ten Dos and Don'ts. No holy commandments control *this* foul creature. Just one law: the law of the jungle. And that law is, of course, **there is no law!**

She reaches down.

Her long bony fingers first stroke the chubby leg of Maggie Jones, then move into a pinching position and . . .

Pinch!

Not the kind of pinch-on-the-cheek pinch you might get from an overexcited grandma, nor the sharp, spiteful pinch you might receive from an embittered older sibling. This was a fingernailed, skin-bruising pinch . . . A pinch cruel enough to wake you from an enchanted sleep.

And, with that pinch, Maggie Jones started to howl. HOoWwwLLLLLLLLLLLL!

It **echoed** around the clearing . . .

It **bounced** between the buildings . . .

It made Mabel's eyes shrink and her teeth

rattle . . .

It made her heart feel like it was being

stretched like **gum** . . .

Pulled from her body . . .

It made her feel like she was going to be

sick . . . so sick!

IT WAS A HOWL THAT COULD NOT BE REFUSED!

Mabel Jones could stand it no more.

'Maggie!'

She pushed her way to the front of the crowd. Her face was red with rage, her eyes filled with tears of injustice. She ran to the centre of the clearing and scooped Maggie up into her arms. 'How could you? She's just a baby!'

The Witch Queen's gap-toothed yellow grin spread from ear to withered ear. 'I've been expecting you, Mabel Jones!'

She signalled to the egret slaves, and the drumming began.

A slow and steady beat.

The Witch Queen giggled. An unusual sound – like the dry crust of a sun-baked cowpat shattering under the heel of a hobnailed boot.

Mabel Jones backed away from the Witch Queen, who began to speak.

'Foul creepers of the jungle undergrowth . . .'

Mabel blinked.

'Rise from the soil . . .'

Mabel gulped.

'Fetch me the one called Mabel Jones!'

Mabel looked down.

A treacherous vine grew at her feet. It twisted between her ankles and squeezed. Mabel fell backwards, cushioning the fall for Maggie, who was still held tightly in her arms.

Another creeper gripped the chubby-thighed grublet, pulling her away from Mabel Jones.

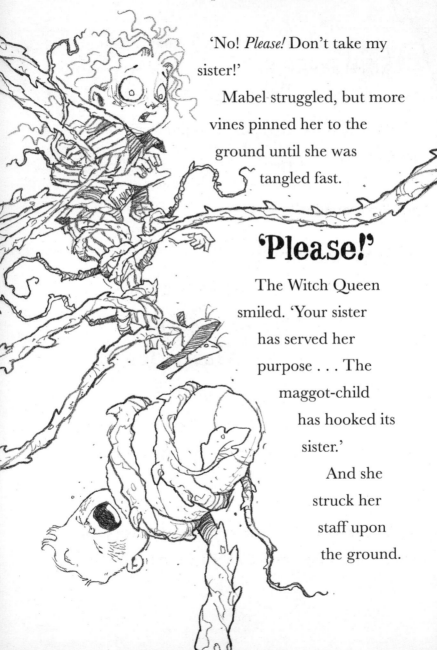

'No! *Please!* Don't take my sister!'

Mabel struggled, but more vines pinned her to the ground until she was tangled fast.

'Please!'

The Witch Queen smiled. 'Your sister has served her purpose . . . The maggot-child has hooked its sister.'

And she struck her staff upon the ground.

'Foul magic of
the jungle soil . . .'

The city began to shake. This time with even
more force.

She lifted her staff to the dark clouds that
swirled around the tower.

'Vile demons of
the forest storm . . .

SEND FORTH
YOUR FURY!'

And at that moment a lightning bolt skittered
across the sky, illuminating the city and striking
the tower.

Blue light danced down the metal skeleton of
the structure. Wood burnt and stone scorched, but
still the lightning jumped and skipped down the

tower. Fizzing
and crackling, it
made one final
leap – to the
Witch Queen, who
was flung into the
air, collapsing in a
frazzling heap, just
metres from Mabel Jones.
The crowd fell silent.

Was she dead?

The heap stood up. Blue light danced around
her eyes and mouth. Her voice crackled and spat.

'I AM MORE POWERFUL THAN I HAVE EVER BEEN!'

The Witch Queen pulled an evil-looking knife from her bloomers. She drew the blade across her palm and a thin line of red appeared.

Blood!

Mabel struggled against the creepers. She rolled and kicked but all she achieved was the attention of another binding vine and the loss of her last fluff-covered jelly baby, which rolled into the dust unnoticed.

'Spirits of the dark jungle . . . LET THE TRANSMOGRIFICATION BEGIN!'

The Witch Queen held her cut hand above Mabel Jones. The other clamped on to Mabel's face, pinching her cheeks together, forcing her mouth open.

A drop of blood gathered on the Witch
Queen's hand.

Larger and larger it grew . . .

Until it was ready to fall . . .

CHAPTER THIRTY-TWO
Sweeties

'Ooh, what's that?'

The Witch Queen stared at the ground next to Mabel Jones.

She moved to look closer and her blood dripped wide of Mabel's mouth, soaking harmlessly into the blackened earth.

A strange look crossed the Witch Queen's withered face as she remembered . . .

The memory was thousands of years old, but it still tasted as if it was yesterday. Hooman children throwing *sweeties* over the side of her enclosure. How lucky those hoomans were to have sweeties in so plentiful a supply they could be given away with such abandon.

How long had it been since she had tasted a sweetie . . . ?

The Witch Queen quivered with delight. The first thing she would do, once she was in Mabel Jones's body, in Mabel Jones's world, would be to eat as many sweeties as she could.

But why wait till then . . . ?

And she stooped, picked up Mabel's last jelly baby in her wizened fingers and popped it into her mouth.

She savoured the flavour of the juicy sweet, slowly chewing and letting its syrup drip over her tongue and down her throat . . .

A delicious sticky, fruity, sickly, burning –
BURNING?

BURNING?!

The Witch Queen gripped at her throat.

'Poison!'

She looked at Mabel with
frightened eyes. 'You have
poisoned me?!'

Mabel struggled free
of her bonds, the creepers
losing their strength as the
Witch Queen sank to her knees.

'No. I didn't poison you. I . . .'

Suddenly a small figure
pushed its way to the
front of the crowd in
a burst of silence.

'It was me. I
puts the poison
on it.'

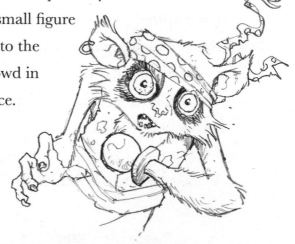

Mabel stared at Omynus Hussh. 'You tried to kill me?'

Omynus shuffled guiltily. 'Only a little bits. I had muddled us best friends as enemies. I thoughts it was you who shots me, not that stinky Count . . .'

Mabel knelt over the dying body of the Witch Queen.

'My life is at an end,' the witch snivelled. 'All I wanted . . . was to be like a hooman snuglet. To have a mother . . . a father. To be loved like a snuglet is loved!'

A tear ran down her cheek. Then she looked at Mabel and snarled. 'And now none of us can live in that world . . . For when I die, so does my magic, and only my magic can summon a porthole to your world.'

The Witch Queen cackled. Her laughter echoed around the buildings of the **FORBIDDEN CITY**, mocking Mabel Jones from all directions.

Mabel drew her cutlass.

'You must help us!'

The Witch Queen shrugged. 'Death holds no fear for me, for I have been dying for many centuries now, and this is surely my last day, whether I die from the blade of a cutlass or pass into a poisoned sleep . . .'

'Then we're **trapped?** Trapped here forever?' asked Mabel desperately.

The Witch Queen grinned wickedly. 'Perhaps not. I have but seconds left on this earth, but you . . . You are young . . . Your body is fresh. Give it to me, and I swear to send your sister home and remain here.'

Mabel gulped. She knew it was the only option. At least that way Maggie could return home, even if Mabel couldn't.

'My name is Mabel Jones, and I am NOT SCARED of ANYTHING!'

Her friends all turned to look at her.

Speke nervously adjusted his monocle. 'I say, Mabel, you're not seriously considering it?'

Jarvis grabbed her by the arm. 'You can't, Mabel. You **can't!**'

'It's the only way,' said Mabel, trying to sound brave but not quite managing it.

She kissed Maggie on the nose and passed her to Jarvis. 'You go through the porthole too. Make sure she gets home.'

Jarvis nodded. 'I promise.'

Mabel stood up and addressed the Witch Queen.

'LET THE TRANSMOGRIFICATION BEGIN!'

CHAPTER THIRTY-THREE
The End

*H*ave **you** ever been pulled from your own body by dark and sinister magic?

You know that part of you that feels **hungry** when you don't eat? The part that feels **sad** when you are alone? The part on the inside that peers from your eye sockets into the outside world? It feels like that part is shrinking – shrinking away to nothing.

As a single drop of the Witch Queen's blood dropped into the willing mouth of Mabel Jones, she felt that shrinking feeling. As the daylight grew more and more distant, she saw faces in the gloom.

Her mum . . .

Her dad . . .

Maggie . . .

And then they too disappeared and she was all alone in the darkness.

It was a most **unlikely** feeling.

CHAPTER THIRTY-FOUR
After the End

*O*h it is a sad day.
A sad, sad day.

A million kitchen towels could not absorb the tears that run down my cheeks, nor a thousand hankies dam the river of snot that flows from my nose.

For those of you who had dreamt of owning a whole shelf of Mabel Jones books, fear not. Copies of my ***HISTORY OF THE PICKLING ONION***, an encyclopaedic series of forty-five books covering pickled onions and their role throughout time, are

unbelievably still available and will fill the gaps in your collection.

Oh, but I would burn them all, every last copy, page by page, to be able to write just one more sentence for Mabel Jones.

Poor sweet, heroic Mabel Jones.

Mabel Jones who made the ultimate sacrifice.

Mabel Jones who, pure of heart, gave herself to save her sister.

What's that you say?

Pure of heart?

Wait!

PURE OF HEART!!!

And now I remember the words of Mr Habib:

'The ultimate sacrifice must be made! Only the pure of heart can defeat dark magic!'

Maybe . . .

Just maybe . . .

CHAPTER THIRTY-FIVE
The Ultimate Sacrifice

*L*ook now, and look hard.

The spirit of the Witch Queen now resides in the body of Mabel Jones. The spirit of Mabel Jones is no more of this world and floats in an unlikely darkness, for a soul without a body to inhabit is mere guff in the wind.

'I'm beautiful!' cried the Witch Queen in the voice of Mabel Jones, running her hands through Mabel's hair. 'I'm young!'

She stretched her supple limbs, tears of joy falling from her eyes.

'I'm hooman!'

She laughed wickedly – not the giggle of a schoolgirl but the cackle of an evil sorceress, and to the watching group who had known and loved the real Mabel Jones it was a grotesque sound.

A sound that showed that Mabel Jones was no more.

Pelf took the pipe from his mouth and shook his head sadly. 'Oh, Mabel. My little snuglet. Ye always were the bravest of us all . . .'

Wiping tears from his eyes, he drew his pistol and pointed it at the Witch Queen. 'Ye'll pay for this, ye withered hag! She was the heartiest of pirates and a **true friend**.'

Jarvis stepped forward, holding Maggie. 'Pelf! No!'

He turned to the Witch Queen. 'It's your turn now! You have to keep your side of the bargain.

SEND MAGGIE HOME!"

The Witch Queen snarled and snatched her staff from beside her old body. She lurched over to a patch of bare earth, unused to such nimble legs. Then she drew a circle in the blackened ground and, with the soft lips of Mabel Jones, spoke a vile incantation.

Slowly the magic circle started to fill with muddy water that bled up from the earth. The Witch Queen stirred it with her staff, and the clouds of silt formed a familiar picture. A messy bedroom, an empty cot and – Jarvis bit his lip to hold back the tears – Mabel's empty bed.

The Witch Queen laughed cruelly. 'Are you missing your friend already?'

She laughed again. And then she stopped laughing.

She clutched her side in pain. 'What's happening? Something is wrong!'

And she's right. Something is very wrong. For, deep within the body of Mabel Jones, an unlikely chemical reaction is occurring. Her kindness gland, engorged by the ultimate sacrifice she has made, is pumping its juices around her system. The dark magic of the Witch Queen is being rejected.

Mr Habib's words ring true: only those who

perform the ultimate sacrifice can be *truly* pure of heart. Only then can dark magic be defeated. For dark magic is old – older than the **FORBIDDEN CITY** itself – and not even the Witch Queen understands it fully. When such power, used for total evil, is countered by total good, then it is nullified, and the natural state of things can return.

Mabel's friends watched as the Witch Queen collapsed to her knees. Falling backwards into the dust, she lay still.

Pelf took a pull from his pipe. 'Aye, it is often the way. The darkness of this most foul deed has led to no good for either of them.'

Then a movement. The twitch of an index finger.

Could it be that . . . ?
Might it be that . . . ?

Can the spirit of Mabel Jones have returned to her body? Or has the Witch Queen's evil soul fought off the goodness that resides inside?

A hand is lifted towards a face.

A groan creeps from between a pair of lips.

Then a finger stretches out and . . .

REJOICE!

Pelf throws his hooves into the air. 'She's picking her nose!'

The crowd cheers in celebration.

'It is her! It is her! Mabel Jones is back!'

Mabel Jones sat up. She looked sheepishly at her friends. 'I was just *scratching* the inside of my nose.'

Jarvis tugged at her sleeve. 'We should hurry.'

He motioned to the magic porthole. It was shrinking! There was no time to lose!

Jarvis handed Maggie back to Mabel and together they stepped forward –

'Wait . . .'

There was a whisper from the old body of the

Witch Queen, kept alive by the wickedness of a final joke.

'I only promised that Maggie could return! As soon as one person passes through the porthole, it will close. If you step through it together, the spell will fail. Two of you – or maybe even parts of *all* of you – will be lost in the steaming mists of time . . .'

The Witch Queen cackled, and the cackle turned to a cough, and the cough to a dying splutter.

'It is my last revenge!'

She coughed once more and then she was silent.

Carruthers checked the body. 'This time she's *really* dead.'

Mabel looked at Jarvis.

Jarvis looked at Mabel.

They nodded.

It was **obvious** who should go through the porthole.

It was **obvious** who needed to be at home the most.

The smallest, most innocentest, never-harmed-anyone person in the world.

Jarvis looked worriedly at the porthole. 'Quickly, it's fading. Bring Maggie!'

Mabel held her sister above the porthole. A vine reached out from the darkness.

'Please take my sister safely home.'

The vine wrapped itself round Maggie and pulled her into the porthole.

Mabel bit her fist as she stared at the image of her bedroom. Seconds seemed liked hours. Her heart thumped in her chest.

'I say!' cried Speke. 'There she is!'

Sure enough, the vine was creeping out of the wardrobe with Maggie wrapped in its firm embrace.

Carruthers scratched his head. 'Well, I must say, this is all *most* unscientific.'

The vine gently laid Maggie back into the cot it had plucked her from all those days before. She snuggled into her blanket and began to snore.

Mabel looked at Jarvis.

Jarvis looked at Mabel.

She was home.

Maggie Jones was really home.

EPILOGUE

*A*nd so it was that Maggie Jones was returned safely home, none the wiser for her adventure. Hooman children remember pretty much nothing of their first few years, being generally short on brain matter, even if they're involved in such unlikely adventures.

Mabel and the others left the ruined kingdom on foot. With the death of the Witch Queen, the egret slaves were freed from her dark magic and the **FORBIDDEN CITY** was once again left to the plants of the jungle. And, as they trekked back to the **BROWN TROUT**, Mabel and Jarvis dawdled behind with Omynus Hussh while he apologized to Mabel Jones for trying to poison her.

'Don't worry, Omynus,' said Mabel kindly. 'I understand. You weren't thinking straight, but it doesn't matter now. We're friends again.'

Omynus's paw crept into Mabel's hand. 'Do you think you'll ever gets home again too, Mabel?'

He blinked, not sure he wanted to hear the answer.

Mabel smiled. 'Yes. I'm sure I will – and Jarvis

too. But there's something I want to find out first.'

'What's that?' asked Jarvis.

Mabel looked back at the last visible sign of the ruined city: the empty tower that grew from the burnt and blackened earth, like the giant gravestone of a lost civilization.

She picked her nose thoughtfully.

'What happened to all the hoomans?'

ACKNOWLEDGEMENTS

Special thanks to . . .

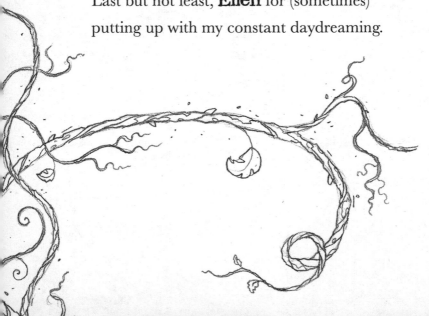

Paul, my agent.

Ross for his amazing illustrations.

Mandy for the great text design.

Everyone at Puffin and Viking, especially
Ben, **Joanna**, **Tig**, **Laura**, **Jacqui**,
Wendy, **Sophia** and **Hannah**.

Big brother **Rich** for all his help and advice.

Mum and **Dad**.

Last but not least, **Ellen** for (sometimes)
putting up with my constant daydreaming.

WANTED

PENNILESS ADVENTURERS
with low moral fibre and experience
of swashbuckling required for
EXCITING OPPORTUNITY
in the field of

PIRACY*

Apply to Capt. Sicklesmear, *The Rancid Tilapia*, City of Dreams
*Must supply own weapons and be weevil tolerant.

QUESTIONS
AND
ARRRRNSWERS!

An interview with the narrator

You've followed Mabel Jones's unlikely adventures closely – have you ever been tempted to help Mabel when she's in a sticky situation?

Yes. I am often tempted to help her. Sometimes, though, I'm too tired. She seems quite capable **(for a booman)**.

Where do you live when you aren't observing unlikely adventures?

I live in many places and in many times. I do have a holiday burrow in the **Upper Jurassic** period. It's a modest hole in among the roots of a fallen ginkgo tree.

What's your grooming regime?

Hygiene is very important to me so I like to take a bath at least once a year. Otherwise it's very simple. Wake, do droppings, bury droppings, lick myself clean, and then I'm **ready to go**. If I'm meeting someone, I might comb some shoulder fur across the hairless patches on my back.

Do you have a best friend?

No. Sometimes I feel very alone.

You've witnessed some pretty hairy moments – what's the scariest situation you've ever been in?

Being accidently stuffed in a **build-a-bear workshop** was quite painful. The extinction of the hooman race comes a close second.

Have you ever actually met Mabel Jones or do you just follow her around?

I like to watch all the major events throughout the history of the world (sometimes more than once). It just so happens that Mabel Jones is present at most of the important ones.

What sort of animal are you?

Labels are for jars of **pickled onions**.

JOIN THE CREW!

Take the **quiz** below and find out which **character** you are most like.

On a ship, where are you most likely to be found?

A. At the helm, making sure we steer clear of rocks and tantalizing mermaids.

B. At the prow, glaring broodily at the sea.

C. On my own in a dark corner.

D. Entertaining my crewmates with stories of past adventures and the occasional romantic sonnet.

What is your most prized treasure?

A. Treasure? Alas, it slips through my fingers like seawater.

B. Treasure is a means to an end, and that end is POWER.

C. Solitude is worth more than any precious gemstone.

D. I'm rich enough. It's excitement I seek.

What is your favourite phrase?

A. 'My body is a temple.'

B. 'I'll tie ye to a carnivorous squid!'

C. I don't speak unless it's totally necessary.

D. 'Ahoy, me hearties!'

If you weren't a pirate, you'd secretly like to . . .

A. Own a small farm on a snowy mountainside.

B. Silence, you mutinous dog! I'll be a pirate until the sea runs dry.

C. But I can't do anything else.

D. Be on stage. Playing Hamlet.

What is your perfect pirate accessory?

A. A pipe and a leather pouch full of rancid tobacco.

B. A rusty cutlass.

C. A sack for loot.

D. An accordion.

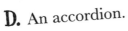

Mostly A:

You are Pelf: captain of the *Brown Trout*. You are worldly and wise, and people often turn to you for advice.

Mostly B:

You are Idryss Ebeneezer Split: captain of the *Feroshus Maggot*. Evil and ferocious, you always get what you want and don't mind crushing anyone in your path.

Mostly C:

You are Omynus Hussh: chief child bagger. You're as quiet as a peanut and as sneaky as a woodlouse in a jar of raisins.

Mostly D:

You are Milton Melton-Mowbray: trainee pirate. You're kind, caring and always coming up with creative ways to entertain friends and family.

Are you ready for a NEW ADVENTURE?

MABEL JONES

and the

DOOMSDAY BOOK

OUT 6 OCTOBER 2016!

Shhh! Listen!

IT'S THE UNLIKELY ADVENTURES OF MABEL JONES

on audiobook!

Out now!

 **Listen**

Do you love listening to stories?

Want to know what happens behind the scenes in a recording studio?

Hear funny sound effects, exclusive author interviews and the best books read by famous authors and actors on the **Puffin Podcast** at **www.puffin.co.uk**

#ListenWithPuffin

Your story starts here . . .

Do you **love books** and
discovering new stories?
Then **www.puffin.co.uk**
is the place for you . . .

- Thrilling adventures, fantastic fiction
  and laugh-out-loud fun

- Brilliant videos featuring your favourite authors
  and characters

- Exciting competitions, news, activities,
  the Puffin blog and SO MUCH more . . .

www.puffin.co.uk

It all started with a Scarecrow

Puffin is over seventy years old.
Sounds ancient, doesn't it? But Puffin has never been
so lively. We're always on the lookout for the next big
idea, which is how it began all those years ago.

Penguin Books was a big idea from the mind of
a man called Allen Lane, who in 1935 invented
the quality paperback and changed the world.
**And from great Penguins, great Puffins grew,
changing the face of children's books forever.**

The first four Puffin Picture Books were hatched in 1940 and the
first Puffin story book featured a man with broomstick arms called
Worzel Gummidge. In 1967 Kaye Webb, Puffin Editor, started the
Puffin Club, promising to **'make children into readers'**.
She kept that promise and over 200,000 children became devoted
Puffineers through their quarterly instalments of *Puffin Post*.

Many years from now, we hope you'll look back and
remember Puffin with a smile. **No matter what your age
or what you're into, there's a Puffin for everyone.**
The possibilities are endless, but one thing is for sure:
whether it's a picture book or a paperback, a sticker book
or a hardback, **if it's got that little Puffin
on it – it's bound to be good.**